The World is Angry

By

John Vines

Contents

Houston

It had been nearly two years since I arrived in Houston. I was approaching thirty then, and until that moment, my world had been North Carolina its landscapes, its people, its familiar rhythms. I suppose most people prefer to stay where they were raised, surrounded by family and friends, where the predictability of daily life offers a kind of comfort. But for me, staying put was never a real option.

The job offer changed everything. It was an opportunity I wouldn't have had otherwise, not in my home state. And once I made the decision, I was resolute. I left everything behind not just my past, but any notion of looking back. There was no safety net, no contingency plan. Only the road ahead.

Independence wasn't just a trait of mine; it was my armor. I could go weeks, even months, without speaking to my mother not out of resentment, but because solitude had become second nature. I liked the quiet, the stillness of my own mind. Perhaps too much. Even now, I can't say whether that detachment was a strength or a flaw. But before I let myself spiral into self-reflection; I should begin with what brought me to Houston in the first place.

Houston was more than a city; it was the center of gravity for the oil and gas industry, a place where fortunes were made from what lay hidden beneath the earth. And I armed with a graduate degree in Geology had finally found my way into that world. Back in North Carolina, my career options were limited. Oil and gas were practically nonexistent, and the thought of spending my life in a classroom, teaching geology, felt suffocating. I wanted more.

Timing had been on my side. In early 2012, the industry was in a hiring frenzy, eager for geologists to chase untapped reserves. The uncertainty of my childhood had taught me one thing: opportunities were rare, and when one appeared, you took it. No hesitation. No second-guessing.

So, when the offer came, I grabbed it. It was more money than I had ever expected to earn, a number so large it didn't feel real at first. But more than that, it was a lifeline proof that I had made it out, that I had secured a future of my own making. Hope. That's what I had felt. Not just for a paycheck, but for a life I had yet to define.

After settling in Texas, I quickly realized that work wasn't just a job it was a routine, one I'd have to adjust to for the rest of my life. Up until then, my days had been filled with school, where structure existed, but in a fluid, ever-changing way. Work, on the other hand, was rigid. From day one, I found myself locked into fixed hours, staring at a screen, the monotony stretching before me like an unending road.

At first, I worked fast too fast. I completed my tasks efficiently, only to realize I was expected to fill an entire eight-hour workday. It didn't take long to notice that no one else worked at full speed all the time. Observing my coworkers, I learned an unspoken rule of the professional world: pace yourself. No one needed the full eight hours to complete their work, so people found ways to stretch it chatting, taking breaks, making rounds. Work wasn't just about productivity; it was about survival.

As children, we move freely between activities, letting curiosity guide our focus. Yet as adults, we're expected to fixate on one thing our jobs for most of our waking hours. How is that normal? How does society expect us to thrive under such monotony? I valued problem-solving, loved the challenge of thinking through complex ideas, but I never cared for the formalities the endless explanations of *how* I arrived at a solution and the *process* that led to the end result.

Maybe I should have known sooner that work, much like life itself, was a game one designed to be endured rather than won. In an ideal world, we would divide our time evenly: eight hours of sleep, eight hours of work, eight hours of play. But reality doesn't allow for such balance. Instead, we chase meaning in moments, choosing quality over the sheer quantity of time spent.

Around this time, I met a detective who, like me, had just moved to Houston. His name was Peter Bryers, and he had come from California. In a way, we were opposites one from the West, the other from the East both now planted in the middle of the country, trying to make sense of a city that was slowly becoming home.

A place starts to feel alive once you form friendships, and despite our completely different careers, Peter and I found common ground over late-night drinks. His detective work fascinated me far more than my own desk-bound job ever could. While I had no illusions that my work in geology was thrilling to others, Peter at least appreciated the science. I explained things in a way that made sense to him, drawing parallels between our worlds after all, geology was its own kind of detective work, piecing together the past through clues left in stone.

Peter, however, enjoyed spending time with my work friends for a different reason there were simply more women. His charm and his detective stories made him a favorite among them, though he was always careful about what details he revealed. Before long, Peter and I became a familiar pair at happy hours near my office the geologist and the detective.

It was during one of these nights out that Laura Wilkes started spending more time with us. And as often happens when a woman joins a close-knit group of men, things got complicated. Peter and I noticed the tension early an unspoken rivalry, a quiet shift in the way we each reacted when she was around. We saw it for what it was and decided to address it head-on, laughing over drinks as we made a pact: if we ever found ourselves drawn to the same woman, we wouldn't let it ruin our friendship.

Laura, hailing from New Orleans, had the charm you'd expect from someone who grew up in the South. She was also incredibly intelligent, able to discuss almost anything with ease. And she had a great sense of humor, making it easy to be around her—like we'd known her forever, and she knew us just as well. We fell into a routine of unwinding together after work, enjoying each other's company. I could mention other people we spent time with, but they aren't key to the story I'm remembering now. That's the thing with emotions: when we reflect on moments, we often recall the tastes, smells, and sounds that transport us back. It's in these moments that the faces of those who made lasting impressions come into focus.

Certain moments in life stay with you, vivid and detailed, as if the world shared that experience with you where you can still recall the sounds, sights, and sensations. For me, there were many such moments, deeply personal, that only held meaning for me. But there are global events, too, ones that stick with everyone, where you could talk to others about where they were when it all unfolded. One such moment for the three of us Laura, Peter, and myself came when we heard about a murder in New Orleans. The details stopped us in our tracks. We all remember where we were when we first heard about it. The victim's eyes had been carefully removed from their sockets and sewn into the center of his chest, with a simple programming code underneath: "Hello World." That's when the killer earned the name "code-blooded killer."

You wouldn't expect one murder to attract so much attention in a world where billions of people go about their daily lives. Hundreds of thousands die each day, often in horrific ways. We live in a system driven by survival, where we try to navigate life, hoping to avoid too much discomfort along the way. So, what made this particular murder stand out? Perhaps it was the media's role in amplifying it. Or maybe, it came at just the right time, tapping into a society already intrigued by such events. Our fascination with murder isn't new, after all—Jack the Ripper's killings are still the stuff of legend, a haunting point of reference for modern crimes.

Laura was the first to truly take notice of the events unfolding. Hailing from New Orleans, she was preparing to return home for the holidays. As we watched the news together, a thought struck me was this killer trying to make a statement with his "Hello World!" message? It was as if he wanted the world to know that he wasn't finished yet. Given the way he staged the crime, it felt like he wanted the body to be discovered before carrying out another killing. The victim's eyes, carefully removed and placed on his chest, were arranged with a precision that made the act feel almost deliberate like a twisted emoji, communicating something chilling: "I'm watching," or "I'm looking for you."

That night, something shifted in the air between the three of us. The conversation slowed, and the familiar camaraderie felt strained. It might have been the unsettling news, or the odd, empty feeling that comes before a trip like the stillness before a storm. Returning home is a bittersweet experience. It's a place filled with memories of your best years, but those emotions can feel distant, almost unreachable over time. The passage of years dulls the intensity of those feelings, leaving you grasping for what once satisfied you. There's a strange anxiety that comes with this the sense that something important has slipped away, leaving you to hold on to the fading echoes of those moments. So, with a mix of quiet unease and a sense of numbness, we said our goodbyes, preparing to head back to our separate, distant homes.

Peter

Peter grew up in Los Angeles, born into a family that embodied the quiet resilience of the lower middle class. His parents, Susan and Tom, were both high school teachers—Susan, with a passion for biology, and Tom, who brought history to life in a way that made the past feel as immediate as the present. Raised in the small town of Bishop, nestled in Owens Valley, Susan and Tom's childhoods shaped them in ways that resonated throughout their adult lives. Although Bishop was a small town of about 5,000 people, its geographical location—tucked between the Sierra Nevada and White-Inyo Mountain ranges—imbued it with a sense of being both isolated and connected to the vast world beyond.

Susan's father, Bryce Mitchell, had moved to Bishop many years earlier, falling in love with the quiet, rugged beauty of the valley. From the moment he arrived, Bryce was captivated by the way the valley's desert landscape stretched out beneath the towering Sierra Nevada mountains to the west and the drier, more desolate White-Inyo mountains to the east. The Sierra Nevada's snow-capped peaks rose as a stark contrast to the arid landscape of the White-Inyos, yet each range held its own distinct beauty.

Bryce's professional life was equally tied to the area. As the director of the University of California's research station in Bishop, he had a unique role—one that allowed him to invite professors and students from California's state universities to explore the natural wonders of the region. For Susan, growing up surrounded by scientists, biologists, and geologists fostered a deep respect for the environment. She heard firsthand accounts of discoveries and research about the desert and mountains surrounding her home.

On the surface, Bishop might seem like a place where little happened. But beneath that quiet exterior lay a world of history and complexity, especially in its geology. The desert, with its seemingly empty expanses, was rich with ancient stories that Susan absorbed with curiosity and awe. The mountains, too, with their ever-changing moods, were never quite the same each time you looked at them. This complexity in nature mirrored the complexities of her own life one filled with contradictions, where the quiet beauty of the valley hid layers of history and knowledge that were just waiting to be uncovered.

It was at the research station where Bryce met Susan's mother, Hannah O'Connor. Hannah, a graduate student studying biology, was leading an undergraduate field class focused on the desert ecosystem. Over the years as the director of the Bishop research station, Bryce had encountered countless researchers, graduate students, and undergraduates. He kept a distance, knowing that mixing personal and professional life could complicate matters, and he was always busy managing the station's operations. But with Hannah, it was different. Despite his usual reservations, he found himself drawn to her—not just for her intelligence and passion for biology, but for something deeper. Hannah was ten years younger than Bryce, but age seemed irrelevant. Their connection was immediate, as if, for a moment, time stood still, and they were simply two people with a shared understanding, unburdened by the usual barriers of age or status.

As their relationship grew stronger, even after Hannah returned to UCLA to finish her degree, she knew that Bishop had become a place where she belonged. The small town, its simplicity, and its natural beauty had captivated her. Bryce had become a part of her life, but so had Bishop. It felt like the right place for her to settle down, and when she heard about a biology teaching position opening up at the local high school, she knew she had to apply. Her qualifications and experience made her an ideal candidate, and she was hired almost immediately. It was as if fate had conspired to bring her back to Bryce and to the life she had come to love. They were married soon after, and together they bought a house in Bishop, starting their new life together. Nine months later, Susan was born, and with her arrival, Bryce and Hannah felt a profound sense of contentment. They had found their place, a life filled with love, a home in a town that was both a sanctuary and a source of endless inspiration.

Peter's father, Tom Bryers, came from a long line of families who had settled in Bishop during the 1850s. His father, Silas Bryers, and his mother, Elizabeth Brown, were part of the town's fabric, deeply embedded in the roles of law and record-keeping. The Bryers family was known for their legacy of sheriffs, passed down through the generations like a rite of passage. The Brown family, on the other hand, had a quieter but no less significant role, serving in the county courts and as the town's librarian. Silas and Elizabeth had known each other since they were children, and their relationship had all the charm of a small-town love story. They were high school sweethearts, destined to marry, and when they did, they envisioned a future where their son, Tom, would follow in his father's footsteps, one day becoming the sheriff of Bishop.

Tom always felt the weight of trying to live up to the expectation of becoming the next sheriff of Bishop, a position passed down through generations. The family often told rich stories of the men who had proudly served the community, but Tom always felt drawn to a different path. From an early age, he preferred his mother's side of the family, spending time in the library or county record office, immersing himself in the stories of people's lives. History became his refuge, and the people from the past became his heroes. While he often heard the phrase, "History teaches us to avoid repeating mistakes," Tom found that history wasn't as simple. It assumes that those who study it will learn from the past, but human nature is often driven by emotion, and decisions are rarely as controlled as we'd like to believe. However, Tom always believed that crime was a reaction to people's emotions in the present, whereas history had rich stories of individuals who triumphed over tragedy and challenges—stories that should never be forgotten.

In a small town like Bishop, everyone knew each other, and there was a sense of mutual respect that allowed people to live their lives with little interference. Tom and Susan's relationship, however, wasn't the typical high school sweetheart story. In fact, they didn't even particularly like each other at first, and more accurately, they simply didn't pay much attention to one another. But one afternoon in high school, everything changed. They were both in the library, studying quietly, when their eyes met. A moment of eye contact, followed by shy smiles, marked the beginning of something new. It was subtle, but sometimes that's all it takes to start a relationship that endures.

When it was time for college, Tom and Susan made a joint decision to stay together and both enrolled at UCLA. Susan's parents were thrilled to see her attend a prestigious university, especially one with strong ties to the University of California system. Tom, however, faced a different situation his family had deep roots in Bishop, and no one had ever left the town. But Tom was adamant about not following in the footsteps of the men in his family, refusing to take on the role of sheriff. Four years at UCLA flew by, and before they knew it, they were faced with the decision of where to live and what careers to pursue. They both fell in love with the energy and diversity of Los Angeles, so they chose to stay. They embarked on careers in teaching, got married, and had Peter, setting down their roots in a city full of opportunity and life.

Peter likely drew on the passions for biology and history that his parents had instilled in him, which contributed to his development as a detective. Growing up in Los Angeles certainly shaped his career path living in a city where crime was a daily occurrence and listening to his parents discuss the latest news over breakfast only fueled his curiosity. But Peter also had a strong connection to Bishop, his family's roots, and the stories his grandfather, Silas, would tell about eastern California's troubled past. These stories were both thrilling and a source of deep pride for Peter, especially one that had been recounted so many times over the years.

One of Peter's favorite family tales was about his great-great-great-grandfather, Paul Bryers, who had played a pivotal role in apprehending the convicts that escaped from Carson City, Nevada, in 1871. A group of twenty-nine dangerous convicts had managed to overtake the guards at the Nevada State Penitentiary and break free. Among them were some of the most vicious criminals of the time, including a gang that became notorious for robbing the Central Pacific Train Line. As with many criminal groups, the sheer size of their number led to chaos, and no one leader could control the entire group.

The gang splintered into smaller bands, with one group led by Charlie Jones, a cold-blooded murderer heading into the rugged eastern California mountains. Charlie, a local of Bishop, was well-acquainted with the area and had even worked there in the past. At first, the authorities weren't overly concerned, leaving the hunt to Nevada officials. But the gang made a fatal error: Charlie shot and killed an eighteen-year-old local pony express rider named Billy Poor. His cold-blooded murder ignited a firestorm of anger in the community, and a posse was quickly formed to track down Charlie and his men.

Deputy Robert Morrison, alongside a local Native American named Mono Jim, led the pursuit. The posse tracked the gang to a nameless lake, where a violent shoot-out occurred, resulting in the deaths of both Deputy Morrison and Mono Jim. This tragedy led Paul Bryers to form his own posse from Bishop. He relentlessly pursued the remaining fugitives and successfully captured all but Charlie Jones. The rest of the gang met their fate on the gallows in Bishop. Though Charlie was never captured, the lake where the shoot-out occurred was named Convict Lake in honor of the fallen lawmen, and the mountains surrounding it were named Mono Jim and Morrison Peaks, memorializing their bravery.

When it was time for Peter to go to college, he initially resisted the idea, wanting to make impulsive decisions about his future. But his parents, understanding the importance of a solid education, wouldn't let him act so hastily. So, he applied and was accepted to UCLA, just like his parents had, and majored in criminology. Peter had always been fascinated by people—he believed that biology, rather than environmental factors, was the primary driver behind our decisions. He felt that the history of human actions, particularly crimes, could offer valuable insights into human behavior.

Peter's path to Houston wasn't complicated, but it was driven by a desire for change and a chance to make a real impact. At the time, Houston was grappling with a surge in crime, and it was on the brink of becoming the new murder capital of the U.S. For years, New Orleans and Chicago had been battling for that unfortunate title, constantly trading places at the top of the list. In cities with stark contrasts in wealth where the rich and poor live side by side and with an under-resourced police force struggling to keep up with rapid growth, violence often finds a way to seep into the fabric of daily life. Houston, fueled by an oil and gas boom thanks to new fracking technologies, was no different. As the city expanded, so did its crime rate, and the police force couldn't keep pace with the growing population and rising tensions.

Texas, and Houston in particular, were fiercely proud of their reputation, and they weren't about to let the crime rate claim a title they didn't want. In response, the city launched a massive recruiting effort for police officers and detectives from across the country. Peter saw this as an exciting opportunity to contribute to something new and dynamic, and to start fresh in a city unlike any he had ever lived in. He jumped at the chance, eager to be part of a solution in a city experiencing rapid change.

Laura

Laura had a natural ability to connect with people, effortlessly fitting in with any group. She had a way of making others feel comfortable instantly, creating space for spontaneous conversation. It was easy to flow from one topic to the next with her, without the tension or awkwardness that sometimes arises when discussing more contentious subjects. But for someone as approachable and easy to talk to as Laura, there was always a sense that you never really knew everything about her. Still, she was a good friend, someone you could trust and rely on, and simply enjoy being around.

Laura's family hailed from Baton Rouge, just north and west of New Orleans. To her, and I believe to me as well, the two cities felt inseparable. The cultural similarities between them were undeniable—the way people walked, talked, and carried themselves seemed almost identical, shaped by the same regional influences. Both cities, founded around 300 years ago by the French, still carried traces of French heritage in their names and cuisine, though they had been thoroughly Americanized over the centuries, blending southern hospitality with language and charm. Laura embodied this southern grace, with a smile that spoke volumes and eye contact that conveyed sincerity in every word.

Her parents, Dean and Mary Wilkes, shared a deep, unwavering love that created a strong family bond. Dean, as the only male in a house full of women Laura, her two sisters, Karen and Amy, and even the dog, Lizzy needed his close-knit group of guy friends. Laura, being the youngest, seemed to inherit traits from both her mother and father, but it was clear she was more sports-oriented, feeling more at ease around men, a result of her close relationship with her dad. Perhaps, being the last child and not the son Dean had once hoped for, he shared his love of sports with Laura, encouraging her in ways he might have with a son. Regardless, there was a lot of love in the family, and Laura grew up feeling connected to her sisters, her mother, and her father in a deep and meaningful way.

We all have a few powerful memories from our childhood that stay with us, shaping who we become as adults. The brain has a curious way of working—almost like it has a routine, pulling up snapshots of past events like a movie that plays over and over again. You could be driving or having coffee, thinking about work or things to do in the present, and then suddenly, your mind shifts, replaying a memory from your childhood. It's as if that moment from the past is reminding you that your history is just as important as the present you're living.

When Laura was twelve years old, she had two best friends who were boys—Jake Tilden and Lucas Williamson. They lived on the same street, so every day, before and after dinner during the long summer breaks, the three of them would run and play for hours. The neighborhood where Laura and her friends lived was different from cities today, like Houston, where homes and backyards are separated by fences, each lawn marking its own territory. It could have been the 1980s or maybe just the small-town nature of the place, but the lawns in their neighborhood seemed to drift into one another, with no real boundary except for an invisible line that marked where one person's space ended and another's began. It was normal to see kids running through yards, using them as shortcuts, responding to the dinner-time whistles from fathers, signaling the end of playtime and the start of a family meal.

One summer evening, after dinner, Laura, Jake, and Lucas gathered again, sitting in Laura's front yard. The hot, humid southern summer nights blanketed their skin in damp heat, and the air seemed to stick to them, forming waves of sweat that beaded on their skin, tracing the contours of their lazy, summer-afternoon hairs. They all anticipated the same thing waiting for the distant sound of the ice cream truck's familiar tune, "Pop Goes the Weasel," as it rolled through the neighborhood. As soon as the music reached their ears, they sprang into action, running as fast as they could back to their houses, yelling for their parents to throw them some money so they could buy ice cream. The mad dash to the front of the yard followed, and in a flash, they had their favorite cold treats in hand, the sweet relief washing over their heated bodies, offering a brief moment of cool comfort on those long, sticky summer evenings.

Laura asked, "You guys know the words to 'Pop Goes the Weasel'?"

Both Jake and Lucas shook their heads. "Nope," they replied, continuing to lick their ice cream, racing to finish before it melted and dripped down their arms.

"Yeah, I thought so," Laura said with a smile. "I only know how to hum the tune, and then I can mouth out the words 'Pop goes the weasel' after humming most of the song."

As the younger kids ran around, screaming and playing tag in the front and back yards, the older teenagers cruised by in their cars, revving their engines as they strutted down the street corners. One evening, a freshly washed and waxed black Mustang slowly rolled down the street, its glossy shine reflecting the dusty orange sunset in the western horizon. That's when Jake and Lucas came up with the most ridiculous, outlandish, and dangerous idea.

"Hey, you losers, your car sucks!" Jake yelled. As he shouted, Lucas gave the teenagers the middle finger. We all burst out laughing, nearly collapsing into the thick, emerald-green grass, unable to control our amusement.

Then, we heard the four scariest words of the night. The driver turned to his friend and said, "Get me my gun."

The moment we heard "gun," adrenaline surged through us. We bolted, running as fast as we could, crossing yard after yard, heading straight for the safety of home. In a kid's mind, the yard is an impenetrable fortress. It doesn't need a fence to define its boundary; it's a space that feels safe from anything that might try to harm you. It was as though that invisible line around our yard shielded us from the world beyond. Once we made it to Laura's front yard, breathless and terrified, the teenagers peeled off in another direction, seeing what trouble they could stir up elsewhere on that summer night.

Laura had been friends with Jake and Lucas her entire childhood, sharing countless memories with them. But that night, the sheer exhilaration of running from the threat of a gun sent a rush of electricity through her body. It was perhaps the first moment she'd experienced with Jake and Lucas that stirred such intense emotions. Those first-time feelings, so overwhelming, flooded her mind, etching into her memory what it meant to be carefree and to experience pure joy in living.

Despite the close bond she shared with them, Laura never developed romantic feelings for either Jake or Lucas. She found more fulfillment in the deep, uncomplicated friendships they had. For most of the guys who came in and out of her life, Laura preferred forming strong, meaningful connections rather than getting caught up in the complexities of romantic entanglements, knowing from experience that such relationships often ended up complicating and damaging the bonds they had.

Me

Personality is one of those traits that stays with us, lingering in our memories long after the details of physical appearance fade away. The way someone looks is fleeting and superficial; we can look back at old photos and marvel at how unflawed our skin appeared in youth, only to compare it with the weathered, drying skin of older years. But personality—that is ingrained, a resonance that remains the same from youth to old age. My mom, Joyce Jenkins, was the strongest woman I ever knew. She was the strongest person I knew even before I could form any concrete memories.

After my mom and dad divorced, she and I grew up together almost like roommates. I was the youngest—my older brother Caleb and sister Jennifer were already living their own lives, finding their own paths. So, it was just my mom and me when we moved from Durham to Chapel Hill, North Carolina. The two towns were only twenty-five miles apart, but in terms of education and the makeup of the community, they were worlds apart.

I quickly realized that the way you speak and the accent you carry can make an immediate and lasting impression. To avoid being mocked or ridiculed, I learned early on how to adapt to my surroundings, even mimicking the way others spoke. Like a snake shedding its skin to begin anew, I learned to shed the old version of myself and embrace a new identity in a new place.

You might think that I would thrive in the new place with all the education being thrown my way, but the truth is, I still had time to ripen and mature, allowing my mind and motivation to catch up to what the world was ready to teach me. I do remember two sets of encyclopedias that I would flip through, mostly reading the words I understood and stopping at the pictures I liked. One set was at my grandmother's house in Trenton, South Carolina, with a copyright from 1954, while the other was in my own home, copyrighted in 1984. Thirty years had passed between those two editions, and a lot had changed in the world during that time science, history, technology, and people doing more and more different things. Numbers and change—those were two ways to look at history: the year as a number and the perspective of events marching along a timeline of inevitable moments. Life moved on, and everything in it continued to occupy space and time in this shared world.

Over the years, my mom and I adapted and pushed through, doing the best we could. If there was one thing I gained from my mom, it was hope and the belief in fairness. No matter how tough things seemed, she instilled in me the belief that hope could help you mentally prevail. With your mind searching and pushing forward, you could move physically toward a path with options. The second lesson she taught me was equality she loved me, my brother, and my sister equally and fairly. To her, there was no other way to be a mom. Even though I was the youngest and likely the spoiled child, both my brother and sister would argue that I was her favorite. But I truly believe that she equalized her love for all of us in a way that felt just and right.

Growing up in a college town like Chapel Hill, I was often told that there were so many options to choose from. But when it came to making decisions about my future, that abundance of choices felt paralyzing. So, as I had done many times before, I adapted and observed what the main group of people my friends were going to decide. Like them, I made the choice to go to college. No one, not my mom nor my extended family, ever directly told me to go. College wasn't a priority in their lives, and they had figured out their own paths. For them, happiness was the goal finding your way in life as long as it brought you joy along the journey.

Real living didn't begin until I left for college, where I finally found my independence. I thought I had figured out what I wanted to do with my life. History was my calling, just like the encyclopedias I had spent countless hours with soaking in what felt like endless, boundless information framed by years and dates. But the reality of time is humbling, and I soon realized my time was limited. I wasn't brave enough to pursue history, though I had loved it. Instead, I ended up taking a geology class because one of my best friend's fathers was a geologist. I never expected it to lead anywhere, but sometimes the things we try without expectation end up being the most important. Out of all the sciences, geology intrigued me the most because it allowed me to investigate the historical record not just the history of humanity, but the Earth's history itself. It was humbling to realize how humans are just a small speck in the vast timeline of events that have unfolded over four and a half billion years.

In a four-to-seven-year span—depending on whether you chose to enhance your learning with a graduate degree you were faced with decisions that would ultimately shape the rest of your life. Childhood and youth offered many flexible paths, where you could wander down different routes without hitting dead ends. You could always return to a familiar path, with as many do-overs as you needed. But as you neared the end of your educational journey, the road became more rigid, with railings that confined you to a laser-focused trajectory. After many setbacks, but never giving up, thanks to the hope my mom instilled in me, I finally made my way out of the only home I had ever known and began a new life in Houston.

Starting a new life was exhausting. It was strange to begin a career only to see those around you leaving and retiring. It felt as if I had just started the race, and others were already crossing the finish line the race I thought we had all started together. I couldn't help but envy those older professionals who were leaving to begin another chapter of their lives. They had "won the race," able to look back and say they had done everything they set out to do. Now, they could do whatever they wanted without being told what to do or where to go.

I'm not sure I can explain it, but it felt like every day was the same—just a dull, gray blur, as if my mind was blank, like a cold, expressionless slab of slate. My mind, like most, craved constant stimulation and new experiences, but I always found myself stuck. I would start new things, thinking I was making progress, but I never truly finished them. Or maybe I did finish them, but only in my mind, where they felt complete, even though in reality, they weren't. Instead, I'd quickly shift focus to the next thing, chasing the excitement of something new.

The real multitaskers used to be called Renaissance men, believed to be capable of anything they set their minds to. We think of ourselves as experts in many areas, leading to inflated opinions that surround us, like an aura as we walk and talk. For me, I was good at geology, but it wasn't a passion. I approached it on the surface, with ideas that seemed clever, but never truly delved deeper. I'd reassure myself that my ideas had already been tested and proven, without bothering to test them myself.

I think that's why I became so fascinated by people their behaviors, their actions. People like to believe they're evolving, changing, but they rarely do. Instead, they follow predictable patterns. Routines become second nature, like rock formations that can be traced to understand how they were deposited over time. One layer after another, stacked up and spread out. The code-blooded killer was doing the same thing creating a trail of murders that marked his thoughts, like tattoos etched on bodies piled up, each one a step in his twisted journey.

The first memories that came to mind when I heard about the killing in New Orleans were of Edgar Allan Poe and the childhood book series I loved reading. As a kid, I was drawn to Poe's stories, perhaps because I didn't have the patience for full-length novels. Short stories and poems suited my attention span much better. I also enjoyed another 1980s children's series called *Choose Your Own Adventure*. What made *Choose Your Own Adventure* unique was its use of the second-person point of view, where the reader was directly addressed as "you," making them the first-person character in the story. What kept me hooked was that at the bottom of each page, I had to choose between two different actions, which would lead me to different pages in the book. It was exciting to jump from one page to the next, rather than reading straight through from start to finish like most books.

The second-person storytelling technique is fascinating, and Edgar Allan Poe used it masterfully in his famous story *The Tell-Tale Heart*. The horror of the story the killing and hiding of the dismembered body under the floorboards grabs the reader right away. But it's Poe's use of "you" that pulls the reader in, making them the first-person participant in the killer's madness and terror. Death has always been a part of human existence, whether through disease, old age, or the tragic results of murder. Humans fear monsters, but haven't we created the monsters that haunt our nightmares? Growing up, I struggled to sleep alone. If I was by myself, I needed a light on and the door closed, just to ease the fears my mind created, imagining all the monsters in the world.

New Orleans

Since the first killing, New Orleans had been on edge, a quiet tension hanging in the air. The French Quarter, as always, remained the heart of the city, drawing both locals and tourists. With its vibrant food scene, lively music, and iconic, walkable streets lined with historic buildings, the area never lost its charm. There was a unique blend of history, where the old and new merged into a tapestry of sights and smells familiar to anyone who had heard of New Orleans. It made sense that a place like this could harbor both the best and worst of humanity in one space.

Laura was particularly drawn to it, as it was so close to home, a place where she had spent much of her life. Peter, already in detective mode, was focused and analytical. As for me, I was the type to become briefly fascinated by anything that caught my attention. Just when you thought the three of us had run out of things to talk about, a new subject would emerge, no matter how dark or macabre it may be. It was easier to discuss when we talked about where the body was found and the condition of the remains. There had likely been hundreds, if not thousands, of serial killers throughout human history.

But it was the killers who left a trail of bodies in such horrifying, memorable ways that stuck with us. The gruesome details of how their victims' bodies were treated seared themselves into our minds. A serial killer is a specialist, an expert, someone with a disturbing focus and a pattern, often targeting a specific type of person. These patterns grab hold of people's imaginations. In society, we admire experts of any kind, those who are exceptional at what they do. If you're good at something, you gain recognition. In the case of these murders, we're trained through stories, movies, and news broadcasts to empathize with the victim, fearing that we could be next, believing that we share some characteristic with those who have fallen prey to these killers.

Most serial killings seem to take place in isolated, eerie locations—like a lake in the woods or a dilapidated, run-down part of a city. But this particular killing, with its fleeting moments of fame, took place in one of the most public places imaginable. The victim was a young white man, wearing a trench coat, slumped over a plate of beignets and café au lait at Café Du Monde, right next to Jackson Square. It almost seemed like he had ordered his last meal before slipping into death's sleep his food left uneaten, still warm on the table. But when the jacket was opened, the victim's eyes stared out from beneath the dark fabric, and the words "Hello World!" were carved into his chest. The killer had made a statement, one that would be remembered with disgust and fear.

The police were baffled, unsure how the victim had been placed in the café, especially with so many people around. It almost seemed as though the killer had a magician's touch. I'm not sure why, but it always seemed to me that serial killers were the true experts able to commit murder and vanish without a trace. Too bad society didn't have more "good" assassins, those who could strike with precision. Is there even such a thing as a "good" or "bad" killer? We tend to categorize everything into black and white, believing that good and bad can never coexist in the same space and time.

Was George wrong to kill Lennie in *Of Mice and Men*? Lennie accidentally killed Curley's wife, unaware of his own strength and unable to control the harm he caused. He never knew when to stop holding on with such an overwhelming grip. George didn't want Lennie to suffer at the hands of those who could only see things in one way good or bad. George knew Lennie wouldn't survive in a world that only made room for one type of man, one type of life. Some aren't meant to live in the imperfect world we've created, even though those flawed people make imperfect decisions in a world filled with imperfect people trying to achieve perfection.

Laura, Peter, and I all agreed that the killer must have half-dragged the victim, with the man's arm around his neck, as if he were too drunk to walk on his own. The French Quarter, with its bustling nightlife and heavy drinking culture, is no stranger to intoxicated individuals, so it's not uncommon for people to see someone helping a drunken companion. Most would have thought nothing of it just another scene of a friend supporting someone who had overindulged. The killer, however, used this as an opportunity to slip under the radar, blending in with the chaos around him.

Once the victim was seated next to the killer, he ordered food and coffee, giving no indication of anything unusual. The food arrived, the coffee steaming in front of them, but the killer didn't linger. After a brief moment, he quietly left, his departure so smooth, so expertly executed, that it was as if he had rehearsed it countless times. Like an assassin who knows how to vanish without a trace, he left the victim behind, unaware that he would soon be discovered by others in the same public space.

You

In the depths of my melancholic mind, I look inward and outward, submerged in a never-ending veneer of shaded blue, a color that seems to echo the sadness and isolation I feel. This world isn't black and white, neatly divided along clear-cut lines. The history of humanity is messy, filled with selfish, self-centered people. In the beginning, things appear beautiful, and we all start off responding to life in ways that bring us the least pain, searching for comfort and ease. Even the worst, most evil figures in history started with good intentions. Even after they committed horrific acts, they still believed some good remained within them. They justified their actions, convinced that both good and bad could coexist and be used to express their view of the world.

The young man in Café Du Monde was just the beginning. It's unfortunate that he had to die for the cause, but once I saw the plan, I couldn't stop carrying it out. I have a one-track mind, incapable of releasing a plan until it's fulfilled. It's just another action among the countless good and bad deeds that occur every day actions people have come to expect. And now, the world will see it in his body.

The eyes he once used had to be removed. Like so many others in this world, he overused them, caught in a cycle of judgment, living through tiny, superficial bites of comfort driven by visuals. Our world has become saturated with cute expressions and empty interactions, all framed by technology. There is no real air to feel on his skin, no sunlight to warm his face where his eyes once saw the purity of light, they now see nothing. Through him, I say, "Hello World!"—welcome to a new era of enlightenment.

Now, the real trick is deciding where to go next. I've already made my mark here in New Orleans, a city that has been my home for as long as I can remember, the place where my story began and where I spent most of my life. It's funny, really how many people end up leaving their hometowns, seeking validation in a place far from where they started, thinking that by stepping away, they will find themselves. Maybe they do. It's all part of the journey, I suppose. But for me, the question remains: could I stay here, in my beloved New Orleans, where I know the streets, the people, the rhythm of life? The answer isn't so simple, though. As much as I love it, there's a part of me that craves more. Like any true artist, I understand that the world itself can be my canvas, and that every living, breathing person is a piece of art waiting to be touched, molded, and sculpted. The world is now watching, and you, too, are waiting to see what will unfold.

This is not just about death; it's about creating something permanent, something that will be remembered. Every great murder, or rather, every great work of art, leaves behind a trail. And this one is no different. Now, my path is set, and I'm walking it step by step. Each move, each decision, is marking the way forward, carving out the story that is yet to be fully told. You can think of this as a game of communication. Each action, every move, is a message—one that's meant to be understood, to make others see the world as I do. There's a reason behind everything, a meaning behind each choice. And even with this newfound relationship between myself and the world, nothing will change the way things are. The bad will always find a way to rise above, casting a shadow over the good, wrapping it in layers of illusion and distraction.

I remember the first time I saw death up close. It wasn't something I was prepared for, not really. It came to me like a scene straight out of a movie. It was a late night, the kind of night that felt like it would never end. We were driving back from my grandparents' house, my dad at the wheel, my mom nearly asleep in the passenger seat, her head resting against the window. I was wide awake, though, staring out the window, watching the world pass by. I had no idea why traffic was so slow that night. It wasn't like there was a rush of cars or anything. But something was off. My dad muttered, "Some kind of accident ahead." I couldn't see anything, but the tension in the air made it clear that something wasn't right. You never really know whether the traffic is slow because the accident is blocking the way, or if it's because people, curious people, are slowing down to catch a glimpse of the wreckage, to see what they shouldn't.

Finally, as we slowly passed the two cars involved in the accident, one image remained seared in my mind, as vivid now as it was in that moment. A man's neck hung limp, angled awkwardly backward, his body slumped downward. His eyes were closed, motionless, and for a brief second, it almost looked peaceful, as if he were merely sleeping. But then, the sight of the blood smeared across his face and down his body—shattered that illusion, replacing any sense of calm with a sudden and overwhelming wave of fear that coursed through every part of me. It was a fear I couldn't shake, and even now, it lingers.

Why is it that some images we see, some moments we witness, stay with us, burned into our memories forever? It's as if the brain can't fully process what it's seen, and so it loops the image, replaying it again and again until we can come to terms with the trauma we've experienced. But no matter how many times it replays, the feeling doesn't fade. It remains, lingering in the corners of my mind, a reminder of that night.

"Would you like to know when you will die?" Laura asked, her voice casual yet cutting through the air like a sharp blade.

"Jesus, Laura, that's direct, isn't it?" Peter responded, raising an eyebrow, clearly taken aback by the question.

Laura didn't seem phased by Peter's reaction. "I mean, wouldn't it be nice to know? That way, you could say your goodbyes, do everything you want, eat, drink, just check off as much as you can before it's all over."

I had just walked into our favorite spot, the bar where we often unwind with beers. There are plenty of great places in Houston for a drink, but after moving to a city of over four million people, it's hard not to feel lost in the endless possibilities. Coming from a college town with only a handful of places to choose from, I found it overwhelming and yet, exciting.

"Laura wants to go crazy before she dies," Peter joked, a laugh escaping him.

"Oh, that's what everyone wants, right?" I quipped back, my voice light.

"It was just a conversation I had with family over the holidays, you know? Talking about the poor guy who was killed in the French Quarter," Laura said, her tone growing more serious.

"You think the killer was sending some kind of message with how he killed that guy?" I asked, my curiosity piqued.

"I don't know. Probably," Laura replied, thoughtfully. "I mean, either you die suddenly, with no time to think about it, or wouldn't it be better to know in advance? That way, you could appreciate life more in the time you have left, knowing it's all coming to an end."

Peter chimed in; his voice steady. "Serial killers definitely send a message with how they kill. It's part of their pattern some twisted way of communicating."

I shook my head, adding, "But we won't know what that pattern is, or what the message will be, until we see the next victim."

Peter paused for a moment, then said, "Taking the victim's eyes out, attaching them to his chest with the carved words 'Hello World' underneath—it's his way of telling the world, 'I'm here, and I have something to say.'"

Laura's voice softened, almost to a whisper, "Someone is going to die next, not knowing when or how. Just like that, their life will be over. Done."

I asked, "You think the killer is going to stay local and kill again in New Orleans?"

Peter shook his head, his voice steady. "Serial killers are always on the move. They're restless, driven by a need to keep moving, part of their infamy comes from traveling, from showcasing their spree like it's a twisted journey."

"He wants his killings to be seen quickly, too," I speculated. "By positioning his first victim in a public place like the French Quarter, he's making sure people notice."

"Exactly! That's why I think he'll move, make his next kill in another public place outside of New Orleans. New Orleans is too risky now, too much attention, for him to display his next victim in a place like that," Peter explained, leaning forward, his eyes intense.

"Yeah, Laura. I think I'd like to know when I'll die," I said, circling back to Laura's original question, the one that had sparked this whole discussion.

"You came back to that," Peter laughed, shaking his head.

"I think deep down, everyone wants to know—wants to understand what's coming, one way or another," I replied, my voice thoughtful.

Laura, usually the quiet one, spoke up, her voice soft. "The guy killed in New Orleans, he knew he was going to die. But waiting, waiting for it to actually happen must have been awful."

We fell silent for a moment, each of us lost in our own thoughts. As we finished our drinks, we sat quietly, getting used to being back in town, back together again. The conversation drifted to other things memories from home, what we missed, what we'd been up to. Eventually, we decided to call it a night.

I still didn't quite call Houston home. Home isn't just a place, it's a feeling. It's that deep connection, rooted in family and friends. It's the small moments that make home what it is: the routine meal you share with family every week, or the first bacon cheeseburger with your best friend after a full day at the local pool. It's when you first saw Raiders of the Lost Ark *with your brother, sister, and dad. There are thousands of these moments, these small, surreal memories of joy, that build up over time and shape the place you belong.*

Here in Houston, I didn't have any of those memories yet. I hadn't yet built that sense of belonging, that community. Houston felt unfamiliar, like a stranger to me, and I, in turn, was a stranger to it.

Scared to death

The gridded streets of Houston make things easier for me, allowing my plans to unfold without overthinking every turn. The simple layout of the city is perfect for my needs straightforward, like the designs I create, quick and deliberate. Hemingway always believed in keeping things simple, direct. There's no need for abstract, complicated layers when plain words get the point across. They'll expect me to move from one area to another for my kills, to keep them guessing, but I'll do it differently. Houston's size, its spread, gives me the perfect cover. It's a sprawling city, a maze of possibilities, far enough from the coastal states to feel more like an interior city. Here, I can appear, blend in, and disappear before anyone has the chance to notice.

Houston, named after Sam Houston, the war hero who fought for Texas' independence. It's amazing when you think about the history, how the two brothers, Augustus and John Allen, chose not to name it after themselves how Allentown could have been a reality. But it probably had to do with their status as outsiders. More likely, though, they were smart businessmen. They named the land they'd bought near Buffalo Bayou after their friend Sam, a move that would define the city's future. Water and land were essential to Houston's rise as a transportation hub. The ships navigated the waterways, bringing goods from the ocean seaport, while the emerging railroads crisscrossed the country, connecting people and trade from all over the United States.

It's fascinating how some cities grow like flowers in the spring—vibrant, thriving, only to wither and disappear by winter. Some winters are so brutal that the flowers never return, and the towns they once bloomed in never see prosperity again. As I drive across this country, I see remnants of these towns, once bustling, now only faint memories. Houston was fortunate, though. It was reborn again and again, most notably when oil was discovered nearby, propelling it to the heart of the booming oil economy. That discovery gave rise to the 20th and 21st centuries' commercial and industrial development. Houston even played a key role in America's leap into space, leading the charge in reaching the moon. Through the years, through the winters and springs of Houston's history, the city's people ensured that it would continue to grow, not only surviving but thriving, becoming influential and important in the world.

The rich have always allowed certain aspects of life to filter down to others in society, but not everything is shared equally. Education is one such vital aspect, one that should be accessible to everyone, to help enhance their lives and broaden their understanding. But art, art was perhaps the first form of knowledge shared with the world. It's the one thing that has always transcended time, allowing humans to capture the essence of living, to take color and shape it into forms that express our experiences. From ancient cave walls where our ancestors painted their lives, their struggles, their survival, art has always been a way to document and honor the moment. In those caves, art wasn't just decoration; it was life and death intertwined. The animals hunted for food; the animals killed to keep life going this was the story the walls told. Art celebrated the struggle, the fight for survival, and the triumph over it.

I will do the same with my art. I will combine art and death, uniting the two into one piece body and skin as the canvas, blood as the paint, and words to express the struggle that defines us all. My art will serve as a statement, a bold proclamation of the reality we face as we move through life, trying to make sense of the chaos and fear around us.

The next piece is already waiting, its form already set. The victim was found last night, a man who had spent his evening in the gambling rooms of Chinatown. His life will become the next masterpiece, the next display for the people to see, to feel. It will strike fear into them this, I know for sure. The people will watch, expecting entertainment from the stream of senseless violence. They consume it the same way they consume everything else, looking through their devices, filtering and distorting their reality, disconnected from true emotions. But this time, it will be different. They will feel fear. True fear. They will be scared to death.

Tantalus

It had been four days since any death connected to the code-blooded killer had appeared in the news. We all knew this wasn't a one-off incident for this serial killer. He hadn't just killed once and been satisfied; it was something more. For him, it was likely akin to a list people make of things to do before they die a series of actions to check off. He had his own list, and with that first kill, he simply marked off one item, knowing that his task was accomplished, at least for the moment. The act of taking a life, to see another person's life extinguished in an instant, that's a different kind of power. It's a reminder of the fragility of life, of how emotions both the good and the bad can be wiped away in the blink of an eye.

But most serial killers can't stop, not once they've tasted that power. After they've gotten away with their first kill, it ignites something deep inside, something that drives them, motivates them to seek more. The kill becomes a cycle. This killer, however, was different. He was patient. He knew that fear was spreading, and with it, the anticipation. People were watching, waiting for the next victim, and in that tension, the killer found his control. The longer they waited, the more fearful they became, and the more powerful he felt.

The police, of course, had no idea where to look. And Peter, with all his experience in analyzing killers, was just as clueless. He'd spent years thinking about the psychology behind murder, yet even he couldn't predict where or when the killer would strike next. The uncertainty of it all weighed heavily on us.

So, when the next body was found in Houston's Chinatown area, we were all shocked. The neighborhood, while still holding the strong presence of one dominant group within Houston, was a place where I rarely felt like a minority. But that feeling was undeniable now, especially as I walked through its streets. Chinatown had changed a lot since I first arrived in Houston. The first wave of Asians came during the end of the Vietnam War, when pro-democracy Vietnamese and Chinese refugees migrated to the United States. But now, with China's rise in affluence, the landscape had shifted again. A new wave of Chinese immigrants from mainland China had come to Houston, altering the very fabric of the neighborhood.

Peter always told me that Houston's Chinatown had many layers to it. Just like the towering buildings downtown that rise section by section into the sky, the one-story shops in Chinatown had layers of their own, stretching deep behind the storefronts and into the hidden alleys. During the day, the streets buzzed with activity, the front of the stores lit by bright neon lights, and customers packed tightly around tables, sharing plates of food. The air was thick with the aroma of sizzling dishes, the steam spiraling upward in winding trails, carrying with it the essence of home-cooked meals and shared moments. But once the stores closed, the atmosphere shifted. The delightful smells of food were replaced by the acrid smoke of cigarettes, curling sideways along the floors, lingering in the air of the crowded rooms where gamblers huddled together, lost in their own world of risk and chance.

I always found it fascinating how crime took root in places like this, where struggle was a constant companion. In areas where life was a daily fight, where survival meant more than just making it through the day, crime felt almost like a natural byproduct. It was raw, immediate, and often inevitable. But even in that chaos, there were rules that organized crime adhered to, ensuring that those who participated could still walk away with their winnings, whatever form they took. That's why, when the code-blooded killer's next victim was found in a Chinatown restaurant, it didn't exactly shock me. It fit the pattern. The killer had already shown a preference for crowded places—his first victim had been found in a bustling area, and now, this was no different.

In some ways, it felt like the killer was deliberately bringing attention to a place of crime we all knew existed but chose to ignore. He wasn't just killing for the sake of it; he was making a statement, pulling the veil back on something we all had suspected but never acknowledged openly. His actions felt calculated, deliberate, like he was trying to expose something that had long been hidden in plain sight.

The first killing had given us a glimpse into the killer's mind—a chilling first impression with the victim's eyes carved out and placed on his chest, accompanied by the haunting words 'Hello World!'. It was a message, one that lingered long after the initial shock. And now, the second victim, a young Chinese man, was found in the same chilling pattern. Like the first victim, he was dressed in a trench coat, an eerie similarity to the young white man found in Café Du Monde. The scene was disturbingly familiar. And when the police opened the trench coat of the dead man, there was no shirt beneath, just the same horrifying markings—something new, something that would speak volumes to those who were paying attention...

2 playing cards – Jack of Spades and Ace of Spades fanned out like a blackjack player

四　死

Everyone　　Tantalus

The first Chinese character was 四, which translated to the number four, followed by the word 死, which meant "die." Below those symbols, the words "everyone" and "Tantalus" were carved with precision. I stared at the markings, feeling the weight of their meaning, trying to piece together what the killer was trying to say. Who was this "everyone" the killer referred to? And why Tantalus?

Tantalus, a figure from Greek mythology, intrigued me. He was a king, the son of Zeus, who had everything anyone could desire—luxury, power, wealth—but it was never enough. Tantalus couldn't stop wanting more. He even thought he could outsmart the gods by serving them the flesh of his own son, believing he could deceive them into eating the child. He also gave humans the gods' nectar, instilling in them an insatiable thirst and hunger for more. His greed was his downfall. The gods, in their anger, punished him severely, condemning him to eternal torment. He would stand in a pool of water with a fruit tree hanging above him, but every time he tried to drink, the water would recede just out of his reach. Every time he reached for the fruit, the branches would lift higher, keeping it just beyond his grasp. It was a cruel cycle: never quite fulfilling the desire, always so close yet always unattainable. The promise of satisfaction, just out of reach, leaving him perpetually tortured by what he could never have.

I pondered this symbolism. Four—unlucky, ominous in Chinese culture, much like the number thirteen in the West. The number four sounds like the word for death, so it's avoided in many Chinese customs. But what did it all mean in relation to Tantalus? A figure cursed to never reach fulfillment, always craving but never able to take. Was the killer hinting at this eternal dissatisfaction, the human condition that so many of us endure, constantly striving for something, but never quite getting it? A chilling thought.

The killer had left his own cryptic message, one that I was still trying to decipher, an invitation perhaps, to understand the mind behind the madness. The combination of the number four, death, and Tantalus seemed to imply something much deeper than just a random act of violence. It felt purposeful. The killer was speaking in riddles, but those riddles were beginning to form a picture.

The next day, Peter and I sat in a coffee shop, the familiar hum of morning chatter around us. The caffeine was slow to take effect, and our minds were still waking up, one sip at a time. We were used to this routine, waiting for Laura to join us, as always, running late. She texted me—"almost there, can you get me a latte?" I looked at Peter, an idea forming.

"Peter," I said, breaking the silence, "how about you do me a favor and grab that latte for Laura?"

Peter raised an eyebrow, smirking. "You're too much. Fine, I'll get it."

Peter quipped, "She asked you, buddy, so get your ass up and order it."

Just then, Laura walked into the coffee shop. Her eyes scanned the room, landing on us immediately. Without missing a beat, she said, "Where's my drink?"

"Getting it right now, my lady," I replied with a grin, feeling the usual playfulness between us.

"Guys don't do anything unless you tell them," Laura teased, her voice light with laughter.

"I heard that," I shot back, smiling.

"Good, I'm glad you did," she said, her laughter bubbling up, filling the space around us.

Peter, never one to miss an opportunity for a jab, smirked and said, "You guys should just get married already. You're acting like an old couple."

Laura looked at him, her eyes narrowing playfully. "I was being serious, somewhat, when I said I have to tell guys to do things. Actually, I've been thinking about something."

She paused for a moment, letting the weight of her words sink in before continuing, "Let's take some time off from work and go after this killer."

Peter and I exchanged a quick glance, processing what she'd just proposed. Then we both burst out laughing, not just chuckles, but real, hearty laughter, as if we'd been drinking. Laura let us have our moment, sitting there with a quiet, amused expression, as if saying, *Are you guys done now?*

Once the laughter subsided, she went on, her tone more serious now. "This killing—it's too close to home for me. It started in my home state, near my hometown, and now it's here, in the city I'm living in."

"Look, we're three smart people. We can figure this out," she continued, her eyes flicking between Peter and me. "Besides, Peter, you've got a gun to protect us if things get hairy."

Her words hit me like a jolt. She did have a point. Part of me was tired of the same routine day in, day out. It felt like we were stuck in a loop, waiting for something to break the monotony. The killer was out there, and this... this could be our chance to make a difference.

I didn't expect Peter to agree so quickly, but I knew how Laura operated. She always got her way in the end. For Peter, it was easier to just go along with her plan and do his best to make sure we didn't do anything reckless. He'd learned long ago that fighting her enthusiasm wasn't worth the energy.

They're still calling me "the code-blooded killer." Haven't they seen my latest piece of art? There's no code on the young man who willingly gave himself to the work of art in my expanding landscape. In time, they will come to understand the meaning, the profound truth they've always known deep within themselves. It's a truth shaped by our shared history of human suffering. How could anyone not understand it, given the lives that have come before us, marked by time and the indelible imprints of history? Yet, they've forgotten. They've become numb to the life we all live, struggling to survive in a world that offers no guarantees.

We're not fighting time itself; we're fighting the very cells inside us—the cells that give us both life and death. From the moment we are born, our cells regenerate, constantly creating new life, even as the old ones die off. At first, the new cells outpace the dying ones, but as we grow older, the balance shifts. The dead cells begin to outnumber the living. The inevitable truth becomes clearer with every passing day. We all succumb to the eternal rest that awaits us. Our bodies, bound by limits, become mere vessels—carrying both life and death in every breath we take.

Icarus

Time is a constant, a thread we return to over and over again. We wake up every morning, finding our way through paths that match our moods, our thoughts, and our desires. Slowly, almost imperceptibly, this creates a routine a rhythm to our lives that marks our very existence. The only true break is sleep, and from the moment we open our eyes each day until we close them at night, we move in a waking state, desperately trying to escape the mundane tedium of living. In each day, there are essentials we cannot escape food, for one. Our bodies demand it, forcing us to follow its rhythms and habits, propelling us from one moment to the next.

And then, in my waking hours, there's art. Art is my break, my escape, my expression. But not just any art—art made from living people. My objects. Sculpted into a state of rest, frozen for eternity, with messages that only the most perceptive can begin to understand.

"So, anyone up for the art museum today?" Laura asked, breaking me from my thoughts.

"Maybe?" Peter replied, unsure.

I looked up. "Sure, why not? Looks like it'll rain today."

"You guys' sound like a fun bunch," Laura laughed. "Look, there's a café inside the museum, and they serve alcohol. We can get a buzz while we look at the art," she continued, eager to sell her idea.

Peter took the wheel today, as we made our way through Houston's sprawling streets, each one flowing into the next like an endless sea of concrete. Strip mall after strip mall—this was the fabric of the city. The scene outside the window reminded me of fog drifting over a dew-covered plain. The city's store fronts, indistinct, lingering like wisps of smoke, blending into the background of the everyday.

In every city, there are neighborhoods defined by the people who live and work in them. Houston, with its vast diversity, is no different. Chinatown is easy to spot, but there are also areas where the Indian, Korean, Russian, and Japanese populations have carved out spaces of their own. These areas, though smaller, are rich with cultural enclaves shops, restaurants, and businesses that blend into the larger cityscape. But Houston's larger Hispanic population means that there's no single, distinct area to call "Hispanic Houston." It's spread across the entire city.

As we drove, the pattern of the city unfolded in front of us. Streets lined with similar shops, one after the other. A whole street, dedicated to lighting stores, all competing for the same customers. It made me wonder: Which store was the first to plant its flag, staking a claim in this part of the city? It's a strange thing, how people always follow what's already been established. If one place proves successful, others will rush in to take a piece of the pie. We even passed two Starbucks on opposite corners, and to make it stranger, there was a Barnes & Noble just up the road, with a Starbucks inside. Within one minute's walk, you could hit three Starbucks. The cannibalistic race to claim coffee customers, all vying for the same dollar.

Once a place is established and rooted to the ground, the area becomes saturated with similar buildings, each contributing to the landscape. The museum district, much like those streets lined with similar shops, was home to several museums all clustered together near Hermann Park. Museums dedicated to children, science, the Holocaust, and art. Even the zoo, while not technically a museum, felt like one to me. Walking through the zoo felt no different than moving from one exhibit to the next in a museum. The animals, confined to their enclosures, became living exhibits for us to observe, just as any artwork would be.

As we approached the art museum, I asked, "Where do we go first?"

Laura smiled, her eyes twinkling as she teased, "You two want your beers first?"

"It's not even noon yet. You think we're alcoholics?" Peter responded, his voice laced with mock offense.

Laura simply smiled at us, her eyes speaking volumes. She didn't need to say a word. Her expression clearly said, *Yes, you guys are functional alcoholics.*

"Well, it is past 11 a.m., and that's close enough to noon," I said quickly, attempting to justify our soon-to-come drink. "Jesus, that does sound like a justifying alcoholic," I continued with a laugh, the humor cutting through the tension.

We hadn't discussed the killer much since we first agreed to try and find him. The silence around the subject was deafening. There's so much to say, but words often settle in the past, resting there without follow-up action. We were thinking about the killer, I knew that, wondering where he might be. Was he still in Houston, or would the next killing be in some other city, broadcast across news networks? The thought gnawed at me as we made our way through the museum halls.

The rooms were filled with art, each piece framed and layered with dark, textured paint. The art spanned centuries—sculptures, pottery, jewelry, portraits of food, people, and landscapes. Walking through the museum felt like stepping through time, each piece a lens into the artist's mind and the era in which they lived. Light danced on the pieces, illuminating the emotions they carried, from vivid portrayals of life to abstract representations of thoughts and experiences.

Every piece of art had a written index card beside it: the name of the work, the year it was created, the artist's name, and the years they lived. Some pieces didn't need much explanation. The artist's name and the historical context were enough to spark the imagination and connect you to the moment in time when the art came into being. The modern pieces, however especially those from the past fifty years often needed more than just a name and a date. Their meaning could only be truly understood with the written "cliff notes" provided alongside them, explaining the deeper layers of the artist's intention.

After visiting the art museum several times, I found myself drawn to the same rooms, returning to stare at paintings that spoke to me on a deeper level. It was like hearing a song over and over again, and with each listen, I marveled at the way my senses formed an attachment to this abstract yet simple creation. There were the famous pieces—the ones you absorb through school and life, through the vast array of information available in the world. Seeing works by Picasso, Van Gogh, Hopper, and others gave me a sense that I understood them completely, almost instinctively. But what if you'd never heard of these artists before? If you saw their artwork for the first time, would it resonate as deeply?

Today, however, I came across something new. A painting called "Approaching High Water" by Karen Gunderson. The piece was painted entirely in black ink on linen, with brush strokes arranged to mimic the movement of waves. What was remarkable about this painting was the way it seemed to come alive as you moved from left to right. The waves shimmered, glimmering in the light as if the artwork itself was caught in the rhythm of a raging storm. All of this, created from nothing but black ink alone, capturing the movement of water with such depth and intensity it was mesmerizing.

Nearby, another piece caught my eye. It was called "Icarus," etched on a copper-green, faded zinc plate. The image immediately transported me to the famous Greek myth of Icarus and his father, Daedalus. Daedalus, an architect and inventor, had been imprisoned with his son inside a labyrinth he had built for King Minos, who had turned against him. To escape, Daedalus crafted wings for himself and Icarus, fashioned from feathers and wax. He warned Icarus not to fly too close to the sun, for the heat would melt the wax and cause the wings to fall apart. But Icarus, fueled by the newfound exhilaration of flight and feeling invincible, ignored his father's advice. He soared higher and higher, drawn to the sun's warmth. As the wax melted, his wings disintegrated, and he fell helplessly into the sea, drowning beneath the waves.

As we stood between these two pieces of art, the weight of their meanings hung heavily in the air. One piece depicted man's overwhelming desires, a representation of ambition and the inevitable downfall it can bring a tragic reflection of human nature, where the climb toward greatness often leads to a devastating fall. The other was a more subtle, yet equally powerful work: it portrayed the shimmering, hypnotic waves of water, captured in black ink, deceptively moving across a flat, two-dimensional surface. The piece played tricks on our eyes, its motion an illusion that felt so real it almost blurred the line between the real world and the art. It made me think about how we, too, as people, sometimes create illusions for ourselves visions of who we want to be, leading us to believe that we are more than what we are.

It was in that moment, as I stood there, contemplating the meaning of these works, that I glanced down at my Apple Watch. A breaking news alert flashed across the screen, the words catching my attention immediately: *Third victim of the "code-blooded killer" discovered.* The sense of dread that had already been simmering in the back of my mind now surged forward, and I quickly tapped the notification.

The third victim had been found in Houston again, this time at the iconic JPMorgan Chase Tower in the Sky Lobby. The news struck with a jolt, sending a wave of unease through me.

The JPMorgan Chase Tower, the tallest building in Houston, loomed over the downtown skyline, its sleek glass exterior reflecting the city's sprawling growth. The Sky Lobby, a public observation deck on the top floor, offered panoramic views of Houston's vast cityscape, stretching out endlessly. It was a popular destination for both tourists and locals who wanted to get a bird's-eye view of the city's skyline. But today, it was the scene of a horrifying crime.

The victim, a male who appeared to be of European descent, was found once again wearing a trench coat. His body had been attached to the glass wall, his arms stretched out as though in flight, the trench coat's sleeves carefully cut into wing-like shapes, creating an eerie resemblance to Icarus. The visual was haunting like a twisted, real-life interpretation of the myth. And just like the previous victims, his chest was marked with cruel precision. The words carved into his skin were chilling: *"Man's desire as Icarus before leads to the fall."* A line was drawn beneath this statement, dividing it from the next: *"Three blind mice at MFAH now."*

Peter, Laura, and I all froze. The instant we read those words; a deep sense of fear took hold of us. We exchanged looks, our skin tightening, and the hairs on our bodies standing up in response. The letters *MFAH* were carved into the poor man's chest marking the Museum of Fine Arts Houston. The words "three blind mice" seemed to be a direct reference to us, the three of us who had just discussed the killer's movements and actions, now standing on the precipice of something even darker than we could have imagined. How could he have known? How could he possibly have known that we would be at the MFAH at that exact moment?

Our hearts raced as the questions spiraled in our minds. The chilling reality of the situation began to sink in. We had become part of the killer's twisted game, and he was watching us, tracking our every move.

Karma

Karma isn't as simple as cause and effect. It's not merely the idea that good deeds bring good fortune or that wrongdoing inevitably leads to suffering. Those notions are convenient illusions mental traps shaped by ancient beliefs, passed down through generations, reinforcing the idea that our present actions dictate not only this life but the next. People cling to these ideas, desperate to find meaning in chaos, to believe in a balance that may not truly exist.

Yet, cause and effect are not entirely without merit. The three men who crossed my path did so through a sequence of events beyond their control a relentless cascade, set in motion long before they ever became aware of it. Their lives unfolded like a row of dominoes, toppling one after another, yet each time they fell, they scrambled back to their feet, determined to keep fighting. They weren't weak-willed; they resisted the current, clung to the illusion of choice. But misalignment is easy to recognize, and once I saw it, there was only one path forward.

Patience is a virtue, but so is precision. I watched. I waited. And when the time was right, I intervened. In the end, their struggles ceased not because of some cosmic retribution, not because fate willed it so, but because I made it so. With steady hands and unwavering resolve, I ensured that they would never rise again.

The young man in New Orleans moved through the world unseen. A shadow. A whisper. A soul unnoticed by those around him, drowning in the loneliness of his own existence. Isolation does strange things to people it carves out spaces in their minds where doubt festers, where self-worth fades, where the need to be heard becomes unbearable.

Observing people has always been my fascination, my silent hobby. I study them, decipher their nature, and predict the choices they will make before they even realize them themselves. But to truly understand someone, distance isn't enough. I have to get close, listen to the moments when they let their guard down. When they are alone, they speak aloud to themselves, as if the buried voices of their subconscious demand release, yearning to be acknowledged.

I am a hunter. Not the kind that stalks the forests for game, but perhaps, in some way, my prey is no different. After all, if you strip away the illusion of civility, what are people but the wildest of animals? Their instincts betray them. Their desires drive them. And if you watch long enough, you begin to see their paths unfold like lines in a story already written.

For weeks, I moved unnoticed through the young man's home, slipping into his life like a specter, studying his habits, tracing the choices that led him here, unraveling the trajectory of where he was headed. Was this what God does? Observing the eight billion souls wandering aimlessly, watching as they stumble through existence, fumbling with purpose, colliding with fate? But I am not as fortunate as God. I cannot simply watch.

I must be patient. I must act.

The young man had made his decision he would end his life. The thought alone should have been enough to consume him, to weigh him down with finality, yet his mind fixated on something else entirely. His appearance.

If nothing else, he wanted to look presentable when they found him. He had no control over the aftermath, no say in how he would be remembered, but he could at least ensure that when someone finally discovered his body, his hair would be neatly trimmed.

A haircut. That was his priority.

One might think that a barbershop would be the easiest place to have a conversation. After all, barbers are professionals at filling silence, skilled at weaving words into the air to smooth over the awkwardness of strangers sitting too close, staring at their own reflections. They are multitaskers in the truest sense able to shape a person's outward image while simultaneously navigating the delicate art of small talk.

Yet, even in this setting, even with a practiced conversationalist nudging him along, the young man struggled. Words failed him. He sat stiffly in the chair, his thoughts a thousand miles away, answering in nods and monosyllables. The moment felt eerily similar to standing in an elevator with a stranger, both obeying that unspoken rule of silence as the metal box carried them upward.

Except for him, there was no ascent. Only the inevitability of the fall.

When Jake woke up, disoriented and bound, he must have thought he was still dreaming. The haziness of sleep clashed with the stark reality of his predicament—his wrists and ankles restrained, tape stretched across his mouth, restricting both speech and breath. Panic flickered in his eyes as he struggled to retrace his steps, to remember how he had ended up like this. But memory failed him.

I watched him for a moment, letting him settle into the weight of his new reality. Then, in a calm, measured voice, I introduced myself.

"Jake," I said, "my name is David."

His eyes darted toward me, wide with confusion. The mind clings to reason in moments like these, searching for a logical explanation. A home invasion? A prank gone too far? The subconscious prefers the absurd over the terrifying truth.

I crouched beside him. "Will you be calm if I take the tape off your mouth?"

A moment of hesitation. Then, a slow, deliberate nod subtle, but unmistakably a 'yes.' A small act of trust. A transaction of understanding.

With that, I peeled the tape from his lips. He exhaled sharply, the sudden freedom drawing in air as if he had been holding his breath for hours.

"What do you want with me?" he asked, his voice raw, laced with fear. "How do you know me?"

I didn't dance around the answer. I didn't coat it in false reassurances.

"I am going to kill you," I said.

His face contorted in disbelief. "What?" The word barely escaped, strangled by shock. "I don't want to die," he whispered, as if saying it aloud might change something.

"Of course you do," I replied, tilting my head slightly. "You were going to kill yourself."

Jake blinked rapidly, his thoughts colliding, unraveling, grasping for meaning. I leaned in closer.

"I know you," I continued. "I've been watching you, Jake. Right here, in your own home, as you sat alone, talking to yourself. You couldn't help it, could you? That need to be heard. Even when no one was listening."

I smiled.

"But I was listening."

"Well, I don't want to die like this," Jake said, his voice quivering between defiance and fear. "I want to go my own way. It's my right my life, my choice." His breath hitched as he struggled against the ropes. "I should get to decide how I die!"

I studied him, amused by his sudden conviction. The will to live is fascinating—it flickers weakly in the lonely, but the moment death becomes real, it burns bright, desperate to stay alight.

"You think most people get to choose when and how they die?" I asked, tilting my head. "If anything, you should be grateful. I'm doing you a favor."

"A favor?" he scoffed, disbelief etched into his face. "How is this a favor?"

"At least I'm taking away the hardest part for you the fear, the hesitation." I gestured toward him. "The uncertainty is gone. You don't have to second-guess anymore."

Jake's jaw clenched. "Still… why me?" His voice cracked slightly. "There are so many people in this city why me?"

I smiled, leaning in slightly. "Can't you see? I'm helping you, Jake."

He swallowed hard, his body rigid, every muscle bracing for whatever answer would come next.

"It's your karma," I said simply.

Jake let out a hollow laugh part disbelief, part hysteria. "Karma?" he repeated. "I haven't done anything to deserve this." His breathing quickened, panic creeping in. "I've never hurt anyone. I've never done anything that"

"Not yet," I interrupted, my voice calm, measured. "But isn't suicide a sin?" I arched an eyebrow. "Isn't it something that condemns you in the next life? Maybe even sends you straight to hell?"

Jake stared at me, his pupils blown wide, caught between fear and confusion.

I let the silence stretch between us before finally whispering, "I'm just saving you from a worse fate."

"What about your karma?" Jake snapped, desperation creeping into his voice. "Killing innocent people who did nothing to you how does that not mess up your own karma?" His breath was ragged now, his panic flaring into anger. "You think you can just do this and walk away clean?"

I smiled, amused by his attempt to turn the conversation back on me. "I don't care about my next life," I said, my voice steady. "I'm not living for some imagined future I'm living for now." I let my words settle between us before leaning in slightly. "And you? You will become a part of my art. In death, you will finally be seen, Jake. A presence, a name, something you've never truly been in life."

That was when I saw it that flicker of recognition, the widening of his eyes when I said *'in death.'* That was the moment he understood. Not just that he would die, but that his existence, insignificant as it had been, was now being shaped into something beyond his control.

And in that moment, I knew.

I would take his eyes.

They would be part of the art I would create, the message I would project through his body. A final display of meaning, carved from his anonymity.

I had once thought killing would be difficult, that it would require something extraordinary a surge of rage, a moment of hesitation, an overwhelming sense of power. But in reality, it was effortless. I moved with precision, with purpose, without hesitation, without emotion. It was almost… mechanical. A routine as natural as breathing.

I had made Jake a part of something greater.

I drew the syringe, filled with a smooth, colorless liquid, and pressed the needle against his skin. Pentobarbital Marilyn Monroe's drug of choice, the same barbiturate used to silence the minds of the restless and lull the suffering into eternal sleep. A drug meant to put down dogs and horses, to quiet anxiety, to grant a deeper, more peaceful slumber.

In Jake's case, it would be his last.

As the substance entered his bloodstream, his body slackened, his eyes fluttering, unfocused. He would never know the full extent of what I had planned for him, but that no longer mattered. He belonged to the art now.

To *my* art.

I had thirty minutes to get Jonathan to Café Du Monde before the pentobarbital fully claimed him. His body was already shutting down, his nervous system drowning in the chemical tide I had unleashed. The brain resists death, clawing to keep the heart beating, the lungs expanding desperately maintaining the rhythm of life even as it slips away. But resistance was futile. His fate had already been decided.

I worked with what little motor function he had left, guiding his faltering steps through the streets of New Orleans. He was just another drunk, slouched in a trench coat, stumbling his way down Bourbon Street, lost to the neon haze and the scent of stale beer. A fixture of the city's nightlife. People see what they want to see. And in a place like this, a man barely holding himself up is nothing out of the ordinary.

His empty sockets were concealed behind a pair of sunglasses. A final touch to preserve the illusion of normalcy. The few passersby who spared us a glance either looked away quickly, uncomfortable in their curiosity, or laughed awkwardly because that's what people do when they don't know what else to do.

Without issue, without suspicion, we reached Café Du Monde and took a seat.

I ordered for him coffee and a beignet. Maybe, if there was anything left of him, this would be his last taste of the world. But his thirty minutes were up, and by then, there was no waking from his sleep. His rest had become permanent.

Soon, his trench coat would be opened.

Soon, the city would see my work.

His own eyes would stare back at them from the center of his chest, greeting the world he had once tried so hard to escape. Hello World! his final introduction, his eternal signature.

My time in New Orleans was over. The gallery of my art here consisted of one piece. But Houston… Houston had *potential*. There were countless options waiting for me, living canvases ready to be shaped into something meaningful.

And then there was *her*.

She thought I had forgotten.

She would soon understand that I never forget.

She would know after Jake was found that I was coming.

In the moment

The Museum and the JP Morgan Chase building were separated by three miles—just a ten-minute drive. A short distance, yet right now, in this very moment, the space between us and the killer felt impossibly thin.

We were minutes apart.

And unlike us, the killer knew exactly where we stood.

Outside, the latest victim loomed above the city, his body displayed high against the sun-warmed glass, sixty stories up. A modern-day Icarus, his fall halted mid-flight, forever frozen in his descent. The morning light cast shifting patterns across the Museum's walls, framing us between two visions of fate Earl Staley's *Icarus*, reaching skyward, and Karen Gunderson's waves of black, shimmering like liquid midnight. Two artists capturing movement and struggle, oblivion and inevitability.

"How about we have a drink now?" I asked. My voice felt foreign, detached.

Laura and Peter exchanged glances before nodding in unison. "Yeah," Peter said. "That sounds about right."

Without another word, we turned back toward the Museum café, our footsteps barely registering against the polished marble floor. The sunlight streamed through the eight-story windows, casting long, delicate beams across the smooth expanse. It felt like walking on air weightless, untethered.

The hushed murmurs of other visitors wove through the space, a quiet symphony of restraint. Conversations were held in soft tones, as if the very walls demanded reverence. Even our own thoughts seemed to quiet, lulled into stillness by the careful, deliberate atmosphere.

Then we stepped inside the café, and it all shattered.

A rush of sound crashed over us voices colliding, laughter cutting through the air, the clatter of plates and chairs scraping against the floor. The shift was abrupt, overwhelming. The moment we crossed the threshold, the weight of sight, touch, and even thought itself was drowned beneath the sheer force of noise.

For the first time in what felt like hours, we breathed again.

"What the hell is going on?" Peter asked, though we all knew the question had no real answer. His voice carried the weight of frustration, disbelief.

He shook his head. "I'm a detective. I've seen some weird shit before, but this? This is crazy."

We all wished for something stronger, something to dull the growing unease clawing at the edges of our nerves. Instead, we settled on two bottles of red wine—small museum café servings, barely half the size of a standard bottle, but enough to take the edge off.

I turned the bottle in my hands, staring at the deep red liquid inside, before finally speaking. "I don't know," I murmured, "this feels more like magic than science." I glanced at Laura and Peter. "It's as if he has a partner someone watching us, tracking our every move, feeding him information in real time. How else could he have timed it so perfectly? His third victim, found just as we were standing here, completely exposed?"

A chill crawled down my spine, the kind that comes unbidden—the prickle at the back of your neck, the eerie sensation of unseen eyes locked onto you, the gut instinct that tells you *run* even when logic insists nothing is there.

We all felt it.

Silently, without a word of agreement, we turned our heads, scanning the café with sharpened, suspicious eyes. Every face became a potential threat. Every casual glance a little too coincidental. The low hum of conversation took on an ominous edge, the rustling of napkins and the clinking of silverware blending into an indistinct murmur of unease.

Peter exhaled sharply. "Laura, you only talked about this with us, right?" His voice was measured, but there was an edge to it now. "I mean, none of us mentioned a word of this to anyone else?"

His gaze flicked between us, searching for reassurance.

"No!" Laura and I answered in unison, the urgency in our voices leaving no room for doubt.

Yet, the feeling remained thick, inescapable.

Someone knew.

And whoever they were, they were watching.

"This doesn't make any sense," Peter muttered, his frustration evident in the crease between his brows.

None of it did.

We drained the red wine far too quickly, the warmth of the alcohol doing little to dull the cold knot forming in our stomachs. Outside, people walked by, cars weaved through traffic, life moved forward with an effortless certainty we no longer possessed. I watched them, wondering what occupied their minds what mundane concerns, what hopeful thoughts, what quiet worries they carried as they carved out their awaited paths through the day.

Meanwhile, we sat here paralyzed.

The killer was always one step ahead, his shadow stretching over every move we made, as if he could see us in real time, predicting our decisions before we even made them. There was no escaping the feeling that he was watching, listening, waiting.

Three blind mice.

That's what he had called us. A nursery rhyme, seemingly innocent, yet laced with something darker beneath its playful melody. Children's songs are often full of danger, warnings woven into their sing-song verses. But why *this* one?

Were we the mice scurrying in circles, oblivious to the blade that awaited us?

Had we underestimated him? Were we naïve in thinking we could chase a serial killer without consequence?

This wasn't just a game to him it was a warning. *There is danger in seeking the truth, especially when the one controlling it has power over you.*

And now, he did.

The fear was settling in, burrowing beneath our skin, creeping into the corners of our thoughts. He had planted it there, and that alone gave him control.

We were trapped in between. Suspended, much like the sky above us—a shapeless mass of gray clouds, neither storm nor sunlight, just an endless stretch of nothing. These kinds of days inspired no one. Not like when the sun painted the sky a boundless blue, or when clouds floated like untouched pillow giants. Not like the days when the heavens darkened into metallic walls, heavy with the promise of rain, their weight pressing down like an omen, leaving the mind dazed, hypnotized by the rhythmic patter of water against glass.

Each day carried its own season, a cycle of shifting moods, the rise and fall of light and shadow in the span of twenty-four hours.

How many days had we spent basking in the warmth of certainty, blind to the storm gathering on the horizon?

And how many more were left before the darkness consumed us completely?

I suggested to Peter and Laura that sitting around wasn't doing us any good. We needed air something to break the heaviness settling over us like a slow, suffocating tide.

We stepped outside, away from the smooth, frictionless marble floors of the museum. Those floors had been as much a work of art beneath our feet as the masterpieces adorning the walls. But the moment we left them behind, the shift was jarring. The ground outside, rough and unyielding, met our steps with the coarse resistance of sandpaper-gritted concrete. The sky stretched above us in an unbroken expanse of dull gray, the air thick and unmoving, carrying no breeze, no relief just a stale, indifferent stillness pressing against our faces.

We walked in silence, our thoughts as blank as the overcast sky.

Approaching Hermann Park, it felt as though we were moving on autopilot, our minds emptied, going through the forgetful motions that often accompany long walks. The kind where memories don't form, where steps blend together, where time ceases to mark itself. It was an odd kind of void consciousness without presence, motion without recall.

Hermann Park, like so many urban green spaces across the country, was designed to be a place where all people regardless of class, race, or background could come together and find a piece of the natural world amidst the sprawl of industry. Central Park had been the first in the United States, a vision of balance between civilization and the wild. Walking through Houston's Hermann Park felt like stepping into that same idea an oasis carved out of concrete and steel, a reminder that even in cities, we crave the open space of nature.

Like a home with rooms carefully designated for sleeping, eating, and entertaining, cities had their own spaces with purpose. Parks were their living rooms places where people gathered to rest their bodies, calm their minds, and momentarily reconnect with something older, something primal.

Peter broke the silence. "Even here, we're being watched."

Laura and I followed his gaze as he pointed upward.

CCTV cameras.

They perched above us like unblinking sentinels, small and unassuming, yet omnipresent. Watching. Recording. A reminder that, in this modern world, true solitude was an illusion.

"You think he's tracking us through them?" I asked, my voice quiet but weighted.

Laura exhaled, considering. "He would have to be a computer hacking expert."

Peter said nothing.

But in that moment, we all knew *whoever* this man was, whatever he was capable of, he was already proving to be more than we had anticipated.

And we were running out of time to catch up.

"Well, he's killing people in public and getting away with it," Peter said, his voice laced with frustration. He exhaled sharply, shaking his head. "You'd think serial killers get sloppy over time reckless after too many kills. But this guy?" He glanced around, scanning the park. "He's getting better. More precise. He knows we're after him."

A thought struck me. "Let's share our locations."

Laura and Peter turned to me.

"On our phones," I clarified. "If he's tracking us, we should be able to track each other. No more guessing where we are."

Without hesitation, we all pulled out our phones, enabling the location-sharing feature. It was a strange thing, technology how easily we surrendered our privacy with a few taps of our fingers, how we could forget what we had allowed, what we had once monitored. It felt like we had become overbearing parents, obsessively keeping tabs on children who had long outgrown supervision.

Then, as we stared at our screens, Laura's expression shifted. A slow, creeping bewilderment crossed her face.

I noticed immediately. "Everything okay?"

She hesitated, then finally spoke. "I still have my ex-boyfriend's location on my phone."

Peter arched an eyebrow. "And?"

"I just I don't remember keeping it. And he never turned his off either."

I smirked. "Guess you've got some cleanup to do on your phone."

But Laura didn't laugh. She didn't even react. Her eyes remained locked on the screen, her breathing slowing as her mind worked through something we couldn't yet see.

It was like watching a machine process too much information at once—time around her seemed to slow, but inside, her thoughts were racing, jumping from one to the next, trying to piece something together.

Then, finally, she spoke.

"The thing is… he's from New Orleans," she said, her voice quieter now, almost careful.

Peter and I exchanged glances.

Laura swallowed. "But his location is showing up less than five hundred feet from us."

Silence.

The three of us lifted our heads, our gazes snapping away from our phones, scanning Hermann Park with sharp, focused stares.

Peter broke the tension first. "You guys' end… okay? Or badly?"

His tone was forced casual, but we all knew the weight of the question.

And the way Laura's fingers tightened around her phone told us she wasn't so sure of the answer.

"Not good," Laura admitted, her voice tight. "At least… he didn't take it well."

Peter and I exchanged a glance.

I exhaled, forcing myself to stay rational. "Are we being paranoid? Or do we really think your jealous ex just happened to become a serial killer?"

Peter didn't answer right away. His detective instincts were already at work, breaking down possibilities, weighing the likelihood of coincidence versus something far worse.

Then, he asked the only question that mattered.

"What's his name?"

Laura's eyes flickered, her lips parting slightly before she spoke.

"David."

Silence stretched between us, thick and suffocating.

The name lingered in the air like a slow-moving storm, shifting everything we thought we knew.

And somewhere, less than five hundred feet away, David was watching.

Waiting.

Confrontation

Fear has a way of creeping in not with the suddenness of a scream, but like a whisper rising from the depths, coiling low before it strikes.

You'd expect it to start in the head, to trickle down like gravity pulling at the body, making it sag beneath its weight. But fear defies gravity. It doesn't settle—it surges. It climbs upward, crashing into the chest, tightening around the throat, paralyzing thought before the mind can even register its presence.

Those who master fear learn to wield it, to let it coil inside them like a spring, snapping them into action. *Fight or flight.* A primal choice, buried deep in the fabric of instinct. The strongest use it as fuel, an energy that sharpens their reflexes and steels their resolve.

I had never been one of those people.

Every time confrontation loomed, I felt it rise inside me, and every time, I ran. It wasn't a decision, not in the way choices are made with careful deliberation. My body reacted before my mind could protest. There was no weighing of risks, no second-guessing. Just movement.

Run.

Because running meant survival.

Because the alternative the possibility of physical pain, of standing in the heat of conflict was something my mind refused to entertain.

I told myself it was logical, that self-preservation was wisdom. But deep down, I knew better. It wasn't calculation. It was instinct. It was avoidance.

It was fear.

And now, as it surged again, pressing against my ribs, clawing up my spine, something inside me whispered:

This time, you may not have the option to run.

Now, with Peter and Laura by my side, I felt something shift inside me.

I didn't want to back down anymore.

For too long, I had lived in the shadow of avoidance, letting confrontation be something I fled from rather than faced. But standing here, with them, I realized that if I kept running, I would never stop. I had to fight not just whatever was coming, but the instinct inside me that had always chosen flight over resistance.

It was ironic, really. I had always told myself I hated confrontation, yet somehow, it always found me. Maybe that was the real truth that I wasn't avoiding it as much as I thought. Maybe I was meant for it, drawn to it, even if I refused to acknowledge it.

Maybe I wasn't who I had always believed myself to be.

The thought unsettled me. Was it possible that deep down, I *wanted* to fight? That the real me had been waiting for an excuse, a reason to let go? It was easy to tell myself I disliked conflict, that I was different from the people who seemed to thrive on it. But looking back, I had always managed to align myself with those who *did* as if I was drawn to the energy of confrontation, even if I never took part in it myself.

I wasn't just avoiding conflict.

I was *hiding* from it.

A closeted confrontationist.

But now, I wasn't alone anymore.

I had Peter. I had Laura. And for the first time, I felt like I had something worth standing my ground for.

I exhaled and steadied myself. *No more running.*

"What's our next move?" I asked.

Peter turned to Laura. "When was the last time you talked to your ex?"

Laura hesitated, her gaze flickering with something unreadable. "About a year ago," she said finally. "Right before I moved to Houston."

The weight of her words settled between us.

And somewhere, out there in the city, David was waiting.

Peter didn't let it go. His instincts as a detective wouldn't allow it.

"Do you think he's capable of being the killer?" he asked, his tone measured, probing.

Laura exhaled, her fingers tightening slightly around her phone. "I don't know what to think," she admitted. "David… he doesn't have to work. He never did. He comes from money one of those people who never had to worry about anything, so he spent his time *learning*."

She paused, as if trying to put something into words that had always lingered at the back of her mind but had never needed to be spoken aloud.

"He believed in balance," she continued. "Mind and body, always striving to better himself. Reading, training, experimenting anything to keep himself from getting bored. He thought the key to life was discipline, that if you controlled your body, sharpened your mind, and shaped the world around you, you could reach some kind of… enlightenment."

She shook her head. "But now, he's *here*. And he's close to us. Too close. Combine that with the fact that someone knows exactly where we are, and, well…" She trailed off, letting the implication settle between us.

It made sense.

Serial killers weren't usually desperate, struggling figures. They had means. Resources. A sense of control, or at least the *illusion* of control. I had never heard of a killer who was poor and lacking access to the tools they needed to execute their plans. They had the intelligence to think several steps ahead, to anticipate consequences and navigate the game they were playing.

And right now, David fit that profile.

Not just because of his wealth, his intelligence, or even his proximity.

It was the message the words carved into the victim's body. *Three blind mice.*

A nursery rhyme. A taunt. A direct reference to us.

And now, of all places, David was here, in Houston, just *feet* away from us in Hermann Park.

It was circumstantial. But when fact after fact begins to build, layering itself into something undeniable, suspicion morphs into something sharper. Something real.

The only missing piece was motive.

Why?

Why would David kill these people?

Had something set him off? Was there a trigger something in his life that had pushed him from discipline and control to something darker, something beyond control?

Did his breakup with Laura fracture something inside him?

It was a dangerous question, one that begged another: Are monsters created by their circumstances? Or were they always lurking beneath the surface, waiting for an excuse to emerge?

We make decisions every day most of them trivial. What show to watch, what article to read, what food to eat. These choices barely register, dissolving into the blur of routine.

But then there are the other decisions. The ones that don't feel like decisions at first. The ones that settle deep inside, waiting to take root.

I thought about Mount Whitney the twenty-six-mile hike I did in a single day, climbing switchback after switchback, cutting through pure white snow toward jagged granite peaks that stretched effortlessly into an infinite cobalt sky. At the time, it was just a challenge. A test of endurance.

But afterward, something had changed.

I knew I could walk twenty-six miles.

And from that single realization, another thought took shape: *If I could walk twenty-six miles, I could run a marathon.*

And so, I did.

The choice to run that race wasn't made in a single moment. It was set into motion long before, in ways I hadn't even realized at the time.

Maybe David's path was the same. Maybe this didn't start with the first kill.

Maybe it started *long* before that.

And maybe, just maybe, we were standing in the middle of a story that had already been written just waiting for us to catch up to the ending.

Reaching the point where one takes another life must require crossing a series of mental gates, each one forcing a confrontation with guilt—guilt that, in the moment of murder, must be silenced, numbed, or simply abandoned.

But the mind never truly forgets.

Everything we do, every choice we make, is stored, locked away in the depths of the subconscious, waiting. We like to believe we move forward, that we bury things deep enough to never feel them again. But at night, when sleep takes over, the mind becomes something else.

A twin existence.

By day, we function—rational, composed, making choices in the light. But by night, the subconscious rises, stirring, processing, unraveling what we refuse to face while awake. It rages, unfiltered, forcing us to confront what we thought was buried.

And if you've killed, truly killed, what happens when the night mind awakens?

There are only two emotions that drive a person to act with absolute motive and purpose: **love and hate.**

Every murder comes down to motive. It's the first question asked in any investigation. *Why?* What compels someone to do the unspeakable? In some cases, the answer is obvious—a fired employee taking revenge on a boss, a jealous lover consumed by rage. The kind of pain that festers, that warps into something uncontrollable.

But pain alone isn't enough.

Most people have been hurt. Most people have, at some point, wished for the downfall of those who wronged them. But there's a difference between a passing thought and an action. The human mind is fortified by checkpoints, internal barriers that prevent us from making decisions we will regret.

For someone to kill, those gates must be shattered.

And only *pure*, unrelenting hate can do that. The kind that festers until it no longer asks permission. The kind that obliterates reason, consuming everything in its path.

I turned to Peter, the question forming before I could second-guess it.

"You think we should tell the police about David?"

Peter exhaled, running a hand through his hair. "I was thinking about it," he admitted, "but I'm not assigned to this case. If I bring someone in and he turns out to be innocent, I could be in serious trouble. And not just me—you and Laura, too."

A pause.

"I can call him," Laura volunteered.

"No," Peter said immediately. "I don't like that idea." His voice was firm, but not dismissive more protective than anything else. "Right now, we can watch him. As long as he doesn't stop sharing his location, we have eyes on him. He probably forgot to turn it off."

For a long moment, none of us spoke.

"So…" I exhaled, feeling the weight of the question pressing against my ribs. "Do we just… go home now? Act like everything is normal?"

If that was even possible.

The silence that followed told me none of us had an answer.

"I think that's our best option for now," Peter said, his voice steady but low, as if speaking too loudly might summon something we weren't ready to face. "Laura can text us his location, and since we all live close, we can act fast if anything seems off. Three against one—we can confront him, but only if it looks like Laura is in danger."

We all nodded, but none of us spoke.

The weight of the night pressed down on us as Peter drove, the silence settling in like an unwanted passenger. It was often like this on return trips—going somewhere always felt different from coming back. There was anticipation in the journey out, a feeling that something was waiting at the destination. Time had a strange duality to it then, stretching thin yet passing quickly with conversation, the miles slipping by almost unnoticed.

But the way back?

The way back was slower.

Without conversation, without the energy of expectation, the distance felt heavier. Every mile dragged, each passing streetlight casting long shadows inside the car. The space between us grew, not physically but mentally, each of us lost in our own thoughts.

When we reached Laura's place, Peter finally spoke.

"Laura, keep an eye on David," he said. "Let us know if you need anything."

She hesitated, gripping her phone tightly before nodding. "I will."

We watched her walk up the steps and disappear inside. The moment she was gone, Peter exhaled, gripping the wheel tighter as he pulled away. The tension in his jaw was obvious, but he didn't say anything right away.

After a while, he glanced over at me.

"Everything alright, buddy?"

I stared out the window, watching the city pass by in blurred streaks of streetlights and empty sidewalks. "I'm not sure," I admitted. "I just… don't know what to do."

Peter kept his eyes on the road. "Look, he knows who we are. He knows we're looking for a killer. But what he *doesn't* know is that we suspect it's him."

I turned to him. "Yeah… I guess you're right."

"If he's watching us, we need to act normal," Peter continued, his voice quieter now, more deliberate. "We stick to our routines. We act like we didn't see the message he left on the victim. We pretend like 'three blind mice' means nothing to us."

The thought settled uneasily in my stomach.

Pretending not to know.

Pretending not to see.

And all the while, wondering if he was out there right now, watching.

"I don't think we'll sleep well tonight," I muttered.

Peter gave me a half-smile, trying to mask his concern. "Try not to worry too much," he said as I stepped out of the car.

But we both knew that was impossible.

As I walked inside, a strange, hollow weight settled in my chest. I had felt alone before, but this was different. It wasn't the solitude of an empty room—it was the loneliness that lingers even when you're surrounded by others.

That kind of loneliness cuts deeper.

It multiplies in the presence of people, stretching itself wide, filling the space between words and glances, making the gap between you and them feel unbridgeable. That was why I had never liked parties. Being in a crowded room while feeling isolated was worse than being alone. It was like sinking into a hole with no way out, watching the world move on above you, untouched by your absence.

The feeling tightened in my chest, pressing against my ribs, as if the very walls around me were closing in. A flicker of panic stirred beneath my skin.

I needed air.

Stepping out into my backyard, I inhaled slowly, letting the night air cool my nerves.

The sky stretched above me, endless and untouched, the moon hanging low a half-circle of soft white, shaped like a bowl filled with the ink of the night, spilling over into an infinite black canvas. The stars pulsed against the dark, scattered like distant, watchful eyes, and a single bright orange dot, Mars blinked among them.

I found Orion's Belt, letting my gaze trace the perfect alignment of the three giant blue stars. There was something grounding in their stillness, in their silent existence across time and space. The air, the vastness of the sky, the sheer insignificance of my worries in the face of the Cosmo *this* was what I needed.

My breath slowed.

The tension in my chest began to ease.

Then, just as I started to release my anxiety, my skin prickled—an old, instinctive alarm, the kind that precedes thought.

I wasn't alone.

I heard it before I felt it the presence of someone behind me, close enough that the air shifted, close enough that my body recognized the threat before my mind could process it.

Then came the blow.

I didn't feel it at first. Just an impact dull and final against the back of my skull. My knees buckled, the ground rising up to meet me.

The stars blurred.

And as my vision darkened, my eyes, heavy as stone, slid shut.

The world is angry

I drifted between consciousness and darkness, my mind sluggish, my body unresponsive. My eyelids fluttered open, blinking slowly, struggling to focus on the blurred, unfamiliar surroundings.

Nothing made sense at first.

The room around me felt foreign, detached from reality, as if I had woken into someone else's nightmare. I tried to piece together the sequence of events, but the only thing that surfaced was the dull, throbbing pain at the back of my skull.

Then it hit me.

The backyard. The feeling of someone behind me. The blow. The ground rising to meet me.

I inhaled sharply, attempting to shift my weight—only to realize I couldn't move.

I was tied to a chair.

The realization sent a surge of panic through my system, cold and immediate. My muscles tensed instinctively, testing the restraints, but they didn't budge. My breathing quickened, my heart hammering against my ribs. For a moment, just a fleeting one, I had been floating in the quiet haze of unconsciousness. But now fear came rushing back, plummeting into me like a body falling from a great height, anxiety crashing down in a freefall I couldn't stop.

A voice broke through the silence.

"So, you're finally waking up."

I froze.

I didn't respond. I didn't even breathe.

I sat there, rigid, motionless, like a deer in headlights, even forcing my eyes to remain unblinking as if stillness might make me invisible. But my body betrayed me in one way I couldn't control: my breathing. Short, sharp puffs, threatening to spill into full-blown hyperventilation.

The voice spoke again, smoother this time. Amused.

"You need to relax," he said, his tone almost *gentle*.

I heard movement, a shift of weight, then "Let's start with introductions." A pause. "My name is David, but you already knew that."

David.

My pulse thundered in my ears. *David. He's here. He took me. This is happening.*

I still couldn't speak. My gaze darted around the room, searching for options, for *something* but there was nothing. No leverage, no escape, no cracks in my restraints. My hands were bound. My legs were locked in place.

David let out a soft chuckle. "And this is where you introduce yourself."

My throat was dry. My mind screamed at me to stay silent, to buy time, to *think*. But my mouth betrayed me before I could stop it.

"My name is Adam," I said, my voice hoarse. "But you already knew that too."

David laughed, and the sound sent a sickening chill down my spine.

"Yes," he said, his voice light, *too* light, as if this were a casual conversation between old friends. "But we can be civilized, can't we? A little formality never hurt anyone."

I swallowed hard, my mind racing.

"If we're being *friendly*," I said, forcing the words past my dry lips, "you should untie me."

David's smile widened, his teeth glinting in the dim light.

"Little mice run," he said, his voice dipping into something darker. "Just like you and your two other mice scurrying, chasing, trying so desperately to catch me."

The air in the room felt heavy, charged with something unspoken.

And for the first time, I realized he wasn't just toying with me.

He was *enjoying* this.

"Yes," I said, gripping onto the last shred of control I had. "They'll come. We're sharing our locations from our phones."

David tilted his head slightly, amusement flickering in his eyes.

"Oh, is that so, Adam?" he asked, his tone carrying that same infuriating air of mock curiosity. "You don't think I *know* that already?"

A pause.

"I stopped sharing your location." His smile widened, his voice smooth, confident. "They have no idea where you are now."

The words landed like a gut punch.

I had nothing left to say.

A silence stretched between us as my brain scrambled for a new foothold, some new angle of escape. And then—*hope.*

A flicker, small but stubborn.

Hope had always been my fallback, my instinct. Even in the worst of times, when life had seemed like a series of dead ends, I had always managed to reframe my circumstances, to convince myself that things could turn in my favor.

For some, hope came from faith, the kind my mother had. She believed in something greater, something unseen, placing her burdens in the hands of God. I had never been able to do that. But faith in *hope itself*? That was something I could grasp.

Hope was limitless.

And right now, that hope had a name: Laura.

She still had David's location. She still had a way to track him. By now, they had to know I was missing. Peter would find me.

David's laugh snapped me back to reality.

"Adam," he said, shaking his head. "I can *see* you thinking."

I forced myself to act casual. "Yeah," I muttered. "I need to use the bathroom."

David smirked. "Really?" He leaned forward slightly. "You sure it's not that my location is still being shared on Laura's phone?"

The air in the room thickened.

That wasn't a question.

It was a statement. A confirmation of what I had been clinging to.

And just like that, hope crashed down around me—sudden, catastrophic, like a stock market collapse after months of artificial inflation.

Hope had always felt like a currency, something people invested in, built up, relied on. But the moment its foundation cracked; it fell apart. The moment the illusion was gone, it became clear it had never been real to begin with.

David let the silence linger, savoring it. Then he spoke, driving the final nail into the coffin.

"Yes," he said smoothly, "that's my *old* phone. The one still sharing its location with Laura." He let the words sink in before delivering the final blow.

"And yes, it's in Houston, just like you thought." A pause. A small, satisfied smile. "But what kind of *thoughtful* killer would be so careless? You really think that's the phone I have on me now?"

He held up another device, casually turning it between his fingers.

"This one right here?" he said, grinning. "Your friends aren't tracking *this* one."

And just like that, the last ember of hope was gone.

This guy had crushed my spirit twice in less than two minutes.

I should have been focused on survival, on finding a way out. But my mind—my mind wandered. Maybe as some last desperate attempt to distract itself from the weight of what was happening.

And now that I thought about it, I was surprised more people didn't kill each other.

Eight billion of us, crawling across the planet, consuming everything in sight, tearing through resources without a second thought. It was a miracle that, across the entirety of human evolution, we hadn't wiped ourselves out—not through war or famine, but by sheer self-destructive impulse.

The mind was the most dangerous thing on Earth.

Not the strongest, not the fastest, but the most lethal.

Animals should fear it.

And people—people should fear themselves.

Because no force in nature caused more destruction, more suffering, than the human mind and its endless capacity for fear, greed, and rage.

I swallowed, forcing myself back to the present.

"So," I said, my voice hoarse, "am I to become victim number four?"

David laughed.

"You think I just kill *random* people?" he asked, his tone teasing, rhetorical.

Something about the way he said it made my stomach twist.

Why me?

Why not Peter or Laura?

I could rationalize why Peter wasn't his target. He was a detective, armed, trained, not an easy mark. But Laura—*Laura was his ex*. If this was about revenge, if this was about anger, wouldn't she have been the logical choice? Wouldn't he have wanted to make her suffer?

Did he choose me because I was the weakest? The easiest to take?

It was a terrible thought, but fear has a way of dragging the worst thoughts to the surface, and right now, my mind was feeding on all the darkest possibilities.

I forced a smile, a pathetic attempt at humor.

"So, you'll let me go then?"

David smirked. "We'll talk," he mused. "Who knows what will happen next?"

Something about the way he said it sent a fresh wave of nausea rolling through me.

"You talked to the others you killed?" I asked, the words slipping out before I could stop them.

"Yes," David said simply. "Just like you would talk to yourself. Or to a friend. Or to an art piece you're working on."

A cold chill passed through me.

This was how I was going to die.

Not in some tragic accident, not from old age or illness, but murdered—at the hands of a serial killer who had, by some sick twist of fate, decided *I* was worth collecting.

No one in my family had ever been murdered. Not even in war. My family followed the *normal* path of dying—old age, disease, the boring, expected timeline of life.

Right now, I *craved* that boring path.

People talk about the 'firsts' to be proud of in a family. The first to graduate college, the first to own a home, the first to make something of themselves.

I didn't want to be the first to be killed.

David leaned back slightly, his gaze steady, as if measuring my reaction.

"I'm not yet inspired to create more art," he said casually. "For now, you're safe."

Safe.

The word rattled in my head. *Safe* was a lie.

He continued, "But I do have a dilemma. You *know* me now. You know I'm the one who killed those three young men."

His voice was calm, almost conversational, as if he were discussing the weather, not cold-blooded murder.

"You have my confession." He tilted his head, a small smirk forming. "But confessions are *slippery* things, aren't they? They can be taken back, twisted, refuted. *He said, she said, et cetera, et cetera, et cetera.*"

His tone was light, almost playful.

"The thing is," he continued, "you and the authorities don't have *evidence* that it was me."

I exhaled slowly.

One would think sitting here, tied up, waiting for the inevitable end, would bring sheer panic. That my body would be trembling with fear, my mind spinning into uncontrollable anxiety, my breath shallow and ragged like someone feverish and drowning.

But instead, a strange calm settled over me.

The kind of calm that comes when you're about to give a speech in front of an audience or take a major exam when you've passed the threshold of dread and stepped into cold, focused clarity. There was no stopping what was coming. That knowledge, in itself, was grounding.

This was survival instinct.

And as I looked at David studied him, watched the way he moved, the way he spoke—I was already thinking about how I was going to get out of this alive.

Then, as if he had all the time in the world, he sat down in a chair across from me and started talking.

David's Story

"Even before I was with Laura," he said, his tone shifting into something more introspective, "I knew there was something *more* I was supposed to accomplish."

He exhaled, running a hand along the armrest of his chair as if the act of speaking required something tactile, something to anchor him.

"I came from a loving, stable family. Money was never a problem, never a stressor. Everything I could ever need was there. There was no struggle, no desperation. But you know what happens when there's *nothing* to fight for?" He glanced at me, as if expecting an answer.

I said nothing.

"You start questioning *everything*." He leaned forward slightly. "Most people don't realize that struggle creates meaning. It *forces* you to define yourself. But when you don't have that—when survival isn't a concern you start chasing something *else*. Purpose."

His fingers drummed against the armrest.

"My parents never pressured me. Never told me what I *should* do with my life. They just assumed I'd figure it out, the same way they did." He gave a small, humorless laugh. "So, I tried. I threw myself into as many things as possible studied everything, learned everything, *did* everything hoping something would *click*. That I'd find *the* thing. The one thing I could dedicate myself too fully."

His voice darkened slightly.

"But you know what happens when you try everything?"

Again, he let the question hang in the air.

I didn't answer.

"You realize you belong *nowhere*."

He leaned back again, stretching his legs slightly, as if recounting an old, frustrating memory.

"Without real pressure, without real stakes, you can't truly *commit* to anything. I spent years searching. Years looking for *that one thing*—something to wake up for, something to *matter*. But every time I thought I found it; I lost interest. I never pushed through, never *became* anything. I didn't belong with the *achievers*, the ones with laser focus, with natural drive.

I just became a *doer*.

A *checklist person*. The type that dabbles in everything but never reaches mastery. The kind of person who learns *just enough* to be decent but never exceptional. I saw those who excelled who *owned* their skill sets, their fields, their passions and I knew, deep down, I wasn't one of them."

He smiled then.

"But then... I found something that *held* my attention. Something that felt different. Something that I didn't lose interest in."

I swallowed; my throat dry.

He didn't have to say it.

I already knew what he was about to say.

And for the first time since waking up in this room, I felt real, undiluted terror.

I spent my time traveling, seeing the world, believing that endless pleasure-seeking would bring me fulfillment. At first, I thought understanding life meant witnessing as much of it as possible, immersing myself in different cultures, landscapes, and experiences. But I wasn't trudging through life the way most people did I wasn't bearing the strain, the weight of survival, of responsibility, of real living. And that realization built inside me like a quiet, gnawing emptiness. The odd thing about emptiness is that it has a weight of its own—just as heavy, just as suffocating as the burden of labor. But where hard work offers release, a moment of well-earned rest before the cycle begins again, emptiness provides no relief. It lingers, an abyss without end, drowning me in a sea of soulless atrophy.

Then I found salvation in art.

I had thought beauty alone the world's most stunning places would be enough. But the people ruined it for me. Books, postcards, and travel brochures sold visions of breathtaking landscapes, untouched wonders, serene, awe-inspiring places. But the moment I arrived; reality shattered the illusion. Crowds swarmed, loud voices clashed, and the sheer weight of human presence suffocated the beauty I had come to see. The postcards should have been honest; they should have included the people, because that was the truth beauty, tarnished by intrusion, wonder, dulled by the inescapable press of the mundane.

And yet, in the midst of my growing disillusionment, museums saved me.

There, in the quiet halls lined with paintings and sculptures, I finally felt free. Unlike the world outside chaotic, cluttered, disappointing art held purity. It was a reflection of history, of human creativity, of something greater than momentary existence. Walking through those galleries, seeing the evolution of form, of thought, of emotion captured in brushstrokes and marble, I realized: this was what humanity was meant for. Not the mindless trampling of beautiful places, but the act of creating something beautiful in itself.

And for the first time in years, the emptiness faded.

Early humans had one purpose finding and storing food. Being warm-blooded was a curse, forcing them into an endless cycle of hunger, search, and survival. Shelter, first from trees, then from overhanging rocks and caves, became their second need, offering protection from the night.

But what happened once those needs were met?

When hunger faded, when bodies were safe, when survival wasn't the only thing consuming the mind what then?

It wasn't enough to simply look up at the stars. No one could resist marveling at them the white, blue, orange, and red glows, tiny glimmers scattered across the blackest sky. The day offered an endless tunnel of blue stretching into infinity, but night was a different kind of vastness a bottomless abyss, punctured with light. And perhaps it was under that endless sky, when thoughts no longer belonged to survival alone, that humans felt the urge to create.

Inside their caves, by flickering firelight, they crushed rocks into colored dust, mixed it with water, and pressed it onto stone. Lines. Shapes. Movement. Life.

The animals that fed them became the animals they painted. The world that sustained them became their art, drawn not in words, but in symbols, in visions. They didn't just survive—they expressed.

And all over the world, tens of thousands of years later, their paintings still remained.

I was trying to follow David's words, his endless ramblings about the world, about meaning, about art. But my mind kept circling one question

Why the hell would he kill for this?

Everyone knew life was tough, fake, a survival game built by other people. But that wasn't a reason to kill.

So, what made him different?

Was he just insane?

Or was there something else?

Some trigger points a single moment that flipped a switch in his mind, turning thoughts into action. A lightbulb moment that led him down this path of death and obsession, where he convinced himself that what he was doing wasn't madness

But art.

"Adam, are you still with me?" David's voice pulled me back.

"Yeah… just processing," I said, though in truth, my mind was racing.

David smirked. "Processing?" His tone dripped with amusement, as if the very idea of struggling to understand was ridiculous.

I swallowed, forcing myself to meet his gaze. "You're smart. Capable. Rich. So why kill innocent people? What did you gain from it?"

David tilted his head slightly, as if considering whether I was even worthy of an answer.

"I didn't kill them to gain anything," he said, his voice calm, deliberate. "Maybe I should start again back to the beginning. Let me tell you why each of them was targeted, why they were made into art, and why I can't stop."

A cold sensation crawled up my spine.

He wasn't going to let me go.

The way he spoke, the ease with which he settled into storytelling—it wasn't the voice of someone who planned to release his audience.

For the first time, I wondered what my last thoughts would be.

I had always imagined that near-death experiences were flashes of meaning, that people saw memories, regrets, lost loves but I was beginning to realize mine would be this. Trapped in a room, listening to a man with a manifesto, a killer convinced his actions were justified.

Maybe these would be the last words I ever heard.

David leaned forward slightly, eyes glinting with something unreadable.

"The first man I killed the one with what the media thought was computer code on his chest? They got it wrong."

I stiffened.

"They assumed I used 'Hello World' to introduce myself to the world," David said, his lips curling into something between a smile and a sneer. "But I wasn't introducing me. I was introducing him."

I frowned.

David's voice softened. "He was a forgotten man—invisible to the world around him. And I gave him an identity."

His fingers tapped idly against the chair's armrest.

"I watch people, Adam. I've watched them my entire life. Observed how they behave. Studied them." His expression flickered with something almost nostalgic. "Sometimes, I learn from them. Like when I was a kid, watching a guy at school land the perfect ollie on his skateboard."

His gaze drifted slightly, as if reliving the memory.

"I was waiting for the bus, and one of the cool kids the best skater in school was doing tricks in the parking lot. And I realized something. I could watch someone, study their movements, and replicate them. Perfectly."

He smirked.

"When I got home that day, I took out my skateboard, twisted my body the way he had—his motions, my motions and just like that… I landed my first ollie."

His eyes met mine again, but this time, there was something darker behind them.

And suddenly, I realized he hadn't stopped learning.

Hadn't stopped watching.

Hadn't stopped replicating.

"The first man I killed was named Jake," David said smoothly. "You probably don't know that, because *she* hasn't told you even though she knows exactly who I killed."

I frowned, but before I could speak, he continued.

"I can see the confusion creeping into your face," he said, tilting his head. "But your eyes… your eyes are lying. They're giving you away. You're afraid."

My breath slowed.

"Laura knew," David pressed. "She was childhood friends with Jake. And she *had* to know I was coming to Houston after I killed him in New Orleans. Why do you think she suddenly came up with this little scheme going after the killer with you and Peter?"

My chest tightened.

"She's *playing* you, Adam."

"What are you talking about?" I asked, my voice sharper than I intended.

David's smirk deepened. "Laura is *using* you. Well mainly Peter. She doesn't want to *catch* me. She wants to kill me."

"That's not true," I shot back. "She's, my friend. She has a good heart. She just she wanted to do something. To stop a killer."

David let out a short, amused laugh. "You're naïve. You never even questioned her, did you? She didn't *ask* you and Peter to go after the killer. She *told* you."

A cold weight settled in my stomach.

"How do you know Laura asked us that?" I demanded.

David leaned forward slightly; his voice soft but charged with something almost *gleeful*.

"I told you. *I watch people.*" He exhaled, as if enjoying the moment. "I was at the coffee shop that morning. I sat there, listening to you three talks about me."

I stiffened. "That's impossible," I said, shaking my head. "Laura would've seen you."

David grinned. "I've killed three people in broad daylight. I've walked among crowds, stood next to police officers, and no one has *ever* seen me. I told you, Adam—I watch, I learn, and then I *apply*." His voice grew more animated, more eager, as if he was *excited* to be explaining this to me.

I forced myself to keep my breathing steady. I had to take control of the conversation.

"Okay," I said slowly, choosing my words carefully. "Let's say, for a second, that I believe you. Then tell me why did you kill Jake? And the others?"

For a moment, David just stared at me.

Then, he smiled.

And I knew he was about to start talking again.

Jake had a good childhood, but he never quite figured out how to transition from a teenager into a man. Life moves in phases, pushing people toward new paths, new identities—but Jake never fully stepped into the next stage.

His best friend, Lucas, and his childhood friend, Laura, had moved on. They took different directions, found their own places in the world. But Jake? Jake floundered. He tried. He really did.

He thought life would just happen that he'd find a job he loved, marry, start a family, just like he had seen others do.

Maybe some people are just lucky.

Maybe the right people just appear like an unexpected spring breeze, brushing across your skin, making you pause, making you feel something. Jake had lost that feeling. And, in truth, he had never given himself a chance to find it again. He didn't put himself out there, didn't seek connection. And when people did come around, he was too shy, too closed off to let them in.

Jake was unknown.

But he wanted to be known to someone, to anyone.

By the time I found him, he had already made up his mind. He was going to kill himself.

And that's when I stepped in.

I had been watching him. Studying him. Hunting him.

The way he would have left this world? It would have been quiet. Lonely. No one would have seen him.

So, I decided to help.

I made it easier for him. I gave him what he wanted.

And in doing so, I started my own path.

I made him seen by the very people who had ignored him.

And I showed the world that I was an artist.

Even as David poured out his reflective confession, I kept searching for logic in his madness.

People justify their actions even when they know they're wrong. And David? He didn't just justify his actions he believed in them.

He was doing horrible things, yet he wouldn't—or couldn't—see his faults. Wouldn't stop himself. The ideas came, and they wouldn't leave until he made them real. And to him, that was proof that they were meant to happen. If something happened, it had a purpose. And if it had a purpose, then it was right.

At least, in a world built by humans.

I had expected to hear something from Laura after Jake's murder. She was his friend. Or at least, I thought she was a true friend. And she knew I was aware of her past of Jake and Lucas.

"You haven't known Laura long enough," David said, his voice laced with something between amusement and pity. "She hasn't told you everything. She can be guarded."

I swallowed, but said nothing.

She never reached out. Not even when I left breadcrumbs for her to follow first, by killing her childhood friend, then by leaving my old phone on, making sure she saw me coming to Houston.

I waited.

And when I got nothing from her, I had another idea.

I put a new plan into motion.

Nick.

A Chinese man I found in Houston's Chinatown.

Slipping into the backrooms of gambling parlors hidden inside Chinatown restaurants was easier than people might think. Secrets never stayed secret for long not when some people just couldn't keep their mouths shut.

My first night in Houston, I was craving Singaporean noodles. Diho Square. A Hong Kong-style Cantonese restaurant with dim lighting, the smell of soy and garlic thick in the air. I knew the place had more to offer the moment I saw they only took cash.

Many old-school Chinese restaurants still operated that way avoiding credit card fees, maybe even skimming a little off the books. Cash leaves fewer trails.

But what really caught my attention?

My waitress.

She was a talker. The kind that filled silences, the kind that wanted to know things. And after a while, between dishes and casual conversation, she finally leaned in and asked

"Are you interested in playing for money?"

I barely had to pretend to hesitate.

Maybe she was told to recruit players for the backroom games, an easy way for the restaurant to bring in extra cash. Either way, I let her think she had me.

I smiled. "I'd like to join."

She nodded, her lips curling into a knowing smirk.

"Come back after 10 PM," she said. "The restaurant closes for dining… but stays open for playing."

When I stepped into the backroom of the restaurant where I had eaten earlier that night, I found myself seated next to Nick and like the waitress, he was a talker.

He poured out his bad luck between rounds of blackjack, lamenting how he was always close to fortune, yet somehow, it always slipped just out of reach. Almost lucky, but never quiet.

Nick talked about everything Chinese culture, Western culture, the philosophies that shaped them both. When I mentioned that I always bet with the number four in mind, he immediately scowled.

"No, that's bad luck!" he snapped. "Four is bad in Chinese. It sounds like 'die.'"

I smiled.

I had always been drawn to Greek myths stories of struggle, punishment, and fate. Even after thousands of years, their lessons still mirrored the harshness of the modern world.

And just like that, I knew.

Nick would be my second victim.

A modern-day Tantalus, cursed to reach for something he could never attain.

Another night, another losing streak at the blackjack tables. This time, I made my move.

I invited Nick back to my Airbnb in Houston for drinks. He was already drunk, drowning in self-pity, and he eagerly agreed convinced, perhaps, that for once, luck had smiled upon him.

I told him he could crash at my place, sleep it off.

Of course, I had other plans.

Nick had spent his life longing, reaching, always denied. But unlike the gods who let Tantalus suffer eternally, I would be a merciful god.

I would finally end his suffering.

I decided to carry the myth of Tantalus into Nick's death.

As I poured drinks bourbon on the rocks I stood behind the bar, preparing two glasses. But along with the drinks, I also prepared a syringe filled with pentobarbital, the same poison that had sent Jake into eternal sleep.

When I placed the drinks down, Nick reached for his—his fingers hovering just above the honey-gold liquid, trapped inside a thick, perfect glass, the oversized ice cube glistening.

I could see it in his eyes the anticipation.

He was already imagining it the first cold touch of the ice against his lips, the bourbon rolling over the cube, cool at first, then warming as it slid down his throat.

A moment of pure indulgence. A fleeting escape from reality.

It never came.

As his hand closed around the glass, I moved.

I clamped his wrist down, freezing him in place.

His eyes snapped to mine, confusion flickering into raw fear.

Before he could react, the needle was already in his skin.

A sharp inhale.

Shock. Realization.

His muscles tensed under my grip, but it was too late.

I watched his eyes as the toxin surged through his veins, his body betraying him, slipping away.

At that moment, I became God.

Nick had spent his life reaching, grasping, always denied.

Unlike the gods who had let Tantalus suffer eternally, I would be merciful.

I would end his suffering.

Back to Reality: The Fear Sets In

David's voice was calm, too calm as he told the story.

But I wasn't just hearing his words I was feeling them.

He wasn't just describing the kill. He was reliving it.

And he was enjoying every second.

This wasn't just murder this was control, a game where he decided when life ended, where he was the sole architect of fate.

David was developing a God complex.

And worse he was thriving on it.

I swallowed hard, forcing my voice to stay steady.

"How did you take the body back to the restaurant?" I asked.

"That was easy. Doors are simple whether you force them open or slip through unnoticed," David said smoothly.

"I went back before 10 p.m., around 9:30, while the front of the restaurant was being cleaned. Employees were taking their smoke breaks, unwinding from their shifts. No one noticed me.

I carried Nick his chest carved, his body a canvas and placed him at his favorite blackjack table. There was a deck of cards sitting there, and I improvised. I opened it, pulled out the ace of spades and the jack of spades, and placed them on his chest, right above my markings."

I was still trying to piece everything together David, Laura, the killings but something wasn't clicking.

There was a missing link, or maybe I was just failing to see it.

Maybe some things aren't meant to make sense.

Cause and effect still ruled the world, but people were unpredictable—complex creatures constantly shifting, their 86 billion neurons firing in endless chaos. With more than 30 trillion cells coursing through our bodies, trying to predict how humans connect, fight, love, and destroy each other was the greatest mystery in history.

David leaned forward slightly; his eyes gleaming.

"Now, let me tell you about my third masterpiece—and how you three blind mice became part of my story."

There was a gleam of satisfaction in his voice, a performer reveling in the unveiling of his work.

It's strange, really how when you position yourself correctly and focus on your craft, opportunities just fall into your hands.

And this one?

Even I couldn't believe how perfectly it aligned.

And, of course it all led back to Laura.

Funny how she always ended up in the middle of everything.

Some people are just like that the centerpiece of the gameboard, the axis around which all the pieces move.

Laura had brought Jake, Peter, and you into this.

And as fate would have it, Lucas was in Houston too.

He became my third art piece.

And yes, I can't forget that I, too, am a piece in Laura's game.

But unlike the others?

I wasn't playing by her rules anymore.

I was revolting.

Lucas and Laura had both come to Houston around the same time, about a year ago.

Yet, despite their shared past, they had drifted into the city as strangers, unaware they were living so close yet so far apart.

People come and go from our lives, but they never truly leave our minds. In the world inside our heads, the past, present, and even imagined futures coexist, shaping us in ways we often don't realize. Memories move us forward, lift us when we're down, or haunt us with regrets, much like waves eroding a shoreline slow, constant, inevitable.

Lucas had an advantage.

His father had long-standing ties with oil and gas executives in Houston—men who had built their wealth over decades. Though his father chose to return to Baton Rouge and New Orleans, preferring to enjoy his fortune where he had grown up, his influence in the industry never faded.

Oil and gas are small world.

Once you make the right connections, you're always part of the club.

So, when Lucas decided to move to Houston, his father didn't hesitate to pull the necessary strings, ensuring his son had a head start in his career.

But even privilege has its limits.

For years, Lucas had felt trapped stuck in the familiar cycle of routine, his world confined to Baton Rouge and New Orleans. He had never stepped outside the sphere of his father's influence, working for the same small company his father had helped run for decades.

Each time the company seemed on the brink of collapse, Lucas's father found a way to save it, pulling solutions out of thin air.

Yet, despite his indispensability, he was never given true ownership—just small bonuses and honorary leadership roles. A savior in the company's eyes, but never its ruler.

Employees admired him, respected him.

But in the end, admiration wasn't power.

And Lucas had spent his entire life living in his father's shadow.

Lucas's father had found his place in the world, not as an owner, but as a respected leader and fixer a man who thrived on solving problems. Respect was his currency, not ownership.

Lucas wanted that too, but he knew he'd never achieve it while standing in his father's shadow. No matter how hard he worked, he'd always carry the stigma of privilege, the unspoken label of someone who didn't earn his position through grit and determination.

Ironically, he never realized his father was still paving his way pulling strings to land him a high-level job in Houston, ensuring he'd start ahead of the pack.

At least here, in this new city, no one knew his father's influence.

No one would brand him a nepo baby.

I narrowed my eyes at David.

"So, you decided to kill another person from Laura's life to hurt her for whatever happened between you two?"

David shook his head.

"No. Lucas was just another stroke of luck. A surreal coincidence."

I scoffed. "Out of four million people, you expect me to believe that?"

"Yes," David said simply. "It's more common than you think.

I've been in New York City, walking down a random street, and suddenly saw someone I knew from college. Nine million people, and yet, there they were.

It's one of the strangest feelings in the world seeing someone familiar in a place where they shouldn't be."

He smirked.

"And now, here I am, crossing paths with Lucas, someone I didn't know personally but because of Laura, his name had always been a whisper in my history."

Maybe David was right.

Running into someone unexpectedly or even hearing from someone you haven't spoken to in years always sends a jolt through your mind.

It's that "Why now?" moment, the eerie sensation that fate is playing some unseen game.

And then there are dreams.

The ones where you suddenly see a face from decades ago someone you hadn't thought of in twenty, thirty years and out of nowhere, they appear.

The subconscious has its own way of working, sifting through the library of stored moments, hidden away in some forgotten corner of the brain.

Maybe coincidence wasn't so random after all.

I wondered what my final thoughts would be when facing death. Would my life's events replay chronologically, each moment soaked in emotion? Or would they appear in random, fragmented flashes, skipping across time in a chaotic reflection of my fleeting existence?

"Hey, Adam the dreamer, you ready to hear how Lucas became my latest art piece for Houston?" David snapped his fingers, pulling me back into the present.

There are rare moments when life aligns so perfectly, when the motions of the day fall effortlessly into place, moving toward a vision only you can see. And then there are the other moments ones where you drift through time, uninspired, trudging forward without direction.

Lucas was one of those perfect accidents, appearing beside me at a bar, quietly sipping his drink. I thought my last art piece the one I had just displayed in Chinatown—had satisfied me. But then there he was, sitting next to me, his face oddly familiar.

At first, I couldn't place him. I closed my eyes, letting the bourbon settle, watching the tiny floating specks drift across the red haze behind my eyelids. And then—like a lightning strike through the dim glow of the bar Laura's face appeared in my mind.

I looked back at Lucas.

"Can you believe this killer out there, doing all this and getting away with it?" I asked, motioning toward the news broadcast playing on the TV above the bar.

Lucas scoffed, shaking his head. "Yeah, messed-up world we're living in," he muttered, almost amused.

"The world is angry," I said, swirling my drink. "People are afraid to even have a conversation now afraid of offending someone, of saying the wrong thing and triggering a fight over beliefs they barely even understand. It's easier to just type something into a screen, pretend that's real interaction. Maybe the world is at its saturation point, killing off its own edges. Or maybe it's always been like this, and we're just now noticing because we're elbow-to-elbow, with nowhere left to hide."

"Huh," Lucas said, slightly tilting his head, trying to understand.

"I'm sorry, my name is David," I said, extending my hand. "Nice to meet you."

"Oh, I'm Lucas. Nice to meet you," Lucas replied, shaking my hand to seal the greeting.

With Lucas, my Greek story continued. And now, my art could tell the tale of Icarus. Just like the complex dramas that have captivated audiences for millennia—from the Greeks to Shakespeare to the present day I knew that after our coffee conversation, you, Peter, and Laura were determined to track me down.

I was like the conductor of an orchestra, and you all were my instruments, following my lead, reacting to my movements, playing your part in the game I had set in motion. I knew you were after me, and I allowed you to think you were getting closer. I deliberately let you believe you were on the right trail, all the while directing your actions to make sure the game unfolded exactly as I wanted.

Lucas's father was the modern-day Daedalus. A man who solved problems but knew his limits, never crossing too far for fear of falling. He had passed that wisdom on to Lucas when he sent him off to Houston live within your abilities, be satisfied with your lot. But children who live in the shadows of their successful but not great fathers always want more. They long to fly higher, to become something greater than what their parents achieved.

Lucas's journey was the embodiment of Icarus he reached too high and fell too far. Leaving his home in Baton Rouge for Houston, Lucas believed he was seeking glory, only to end up drowning in it.

I didn't know how we were going to stop David. Could he even be stopped?

How could anyone, in this day and age with cameras everywhere, constant surveillance, and the eyes of millions get away with murder? Especially in public places? I could understand in isolated places the woods, deserts, or the middle of the ocean. If you didn't have a conscience, guilt, or any moral compass, it would be easy to kill someone just for the experience.

But that's life the decisions we make, the experiences we live through, the choices we have to bear. Some moments are carried out for the experience of feeling and relating them to the greater narrative of life. Yet, it's the living onward with those choices that define us.

The people who carry the weight of their decisions, who live with the guilt of their actions, endure the constant reminder of their mistakes. They wake up every day, passing through the pain each night, only to repeat it the next day. That's life.

And that's the path we walk, from crawling at first to standing in the end.

"You want to know how I was able to take Lucas's body and place it in the sky lobby without anyone noticing?" David asked, eager to share his twisted methods.

"Something tells me you're going to tell me anyway," I replied.

If there's one thing you learn from stories and movies about serial killers, it's that they love to talk, especially when they have control over the place and time. I started wondering where we were. At first, I thought it was some house, but the more I listened to David, the more I realized it felt like an open, endless space, like an office building. More specifically, an abandoned office building which, for a serial killer, is cliché, yet practical. Houston has plenty of downtown office buildings that have remained vacant after companies left. These dilapidated structures of iron, steel, and stone rise like ghost towns stacked on top of each other, eerily silent.

"Houston's downtown is pretty empty compared to other cities," David said, breaking my thoughts. "In places like NYC, Chicago, San Francisco, Seattle, or New Orleans, the downtown areas are alive with people, moving, breaking up their day. But look at us here we're in a building that was once home to one of the largest oil and gas companies in the world. Now it's just a vacant shell empty concrete and windows, taking up space, just like me."

I figured it out. We were in an abandoned office building in downtown Houston. I wondered if Peter and Laura would think of targeting such places empty office buildings where nobody would look. It felt like a long shot, but hope still clung to me, especially with Peter's detective mind. Maybe he was covering every angle, trying to figure out where David could have taken me.

David continued, a strange pride in his voice. "You'd think the sky lobby in the JP Morgan Building would always be crowded with people, like ants in a backyard during summer. But when I brought Lucas there, it was empty. The perfect place to display him like a modern-day Icarus, bathed in the sun's rays, heat shimmering off the two-inch-thick glass sixty floors up. I pretended to be a janitor, stuffing Lucas's body into a rolling garbage bin. With nobody around, I wheeled him out his lifeless body stretched out like a bird, wingless and artistically dead."

I swallowed, the weight of his words sinking in. "Okay, now that you've told me your ways and reasons for killing the three men," I said, trying to steady my voice. "What's next, David?"

"I've told you a lot, yes, but not everything," David continued, his voice smooth. "Don't worry, Adam, I'm in no hurry to end this with you. Not yet, at least. I have time. You have time. But it's limited. Now, we wait for your friends to come and see how clever they can be." His words were calm, but his smile slanted, devilish, and slightly open revealed the darkness beneath his control.

Live as you can as long as you can

Laura paced back and forth, phone in hand, muttering to herself. *Gb*

The doorbell rang.

"Hey, Laura, have you heard from Adam yet?" Peter asked, stepping into her apartment.

"No, I haven't," Laura responded, a hint of frustration in her voice. "I've tried calling him. I saw that his location sharing is off."

"Yeah, I noticed too. He's gone dark. His phone's off the grid, and we can't see his location anymore," Peter said, his voice tight with worry.

"Peter, you think David has him?" Laura asked, her voice trembling with a question she already knew the answer to, but still had to ask.

"That seems to be the only thing both of us are thinking right now," Peter replied, his tone heavy with the same realization.

Laura stared out the window of Peter's car as they drove to get some much-needed coffee after a restless night. Neither of them spoke much. They both felt **numb** to the world around them, each trapped in their own thoughts, unable to fully act or escape the reality of their situation. They never could have imagined this turn of events, finding themselves helpless and paralyzed in the face of it all.

Laura's mind began to drift, her thoughts consumed by memories that flooded in, relentlessly bouncing around her head, trapped within the walls of regret. Regret, she thought, has a way of holding you captive, replaying past mistakes over and over, never allowing you to let go. Does the brain reward both positive and painful emotions? It seems so. For those scarred by life or those who've hurt others, emotions of discontent flow like rivers, eventually forming waterfalls that crash down over us. Over time, these emotional currents erode our souls, using the negative experiences to push us toward moments of relief, whether that relief comes through drugs, alcohol, or a deep sense of redemption that leads to real change.

Laura had been raised differently more like a boy than a girl. She never minded it, even when she saw her sisters partaking in what she considered the traditional "girl things" waiting for friends, constantly wondering what others thought, seeking validation from their peers. In their eyes, life was a competition constantly trying to fit in, desiring the envy of others. But Laura didn't engage in this. She grew up understanding that the first priority in the journey toward acceptance was friendships, even those with people she considered enemies. All of them wanted the same thing: the approval of both boys and girls. The second tier of validation came from family the final circle, where love and approval were meant to feel unconditional. Deep down, however, Laura knew that her family's love was the most important the foundation of her confidence. It was this love that gave her the strength to step forward, to face life with purpose, no matter how flawed or difficult the path seemed.

Of course, Laura experienced all the typical pressures in school, where the division between "girl" things and "boy" things felt utterly ridiculous to her. She bonded with both her mom and dad, but there was something about her relationship with her dad that made her prefer spending time with him. He had a way of completely relaxing and included her in all his activities. They could spend hours together, watching sporting games on TV, and he always made them more than just the sport itself—he told stories about the history of the games and the players, making the experience rich and engaging.

For Laura, finding friends like Jake and Lucas in her childhood years felt natural. Bonding with them was an extension of the relationship she had with her dad. She had already learned to talk and do the things boys enjoyed, from playing outside to exploring new places. The one thing she did inherit from her mom and sisters, though, was that unique switch that women often develop the ability to charm anyone, to make them feel like a friend, but also knowing exactly when to flip a switch and change that dynamic. She understood how to turn on the type of emotional trigger that could shift a man's interest from simple friendship to something deeper, more intimate.

As the three friends grew up, their feelings for each other began to change in ways they hadn't anticipated. Even if they had known that feelings would evolve, they wouldn't have been able to prevent it. It's strange no matter how hard you try to control the course of your actions; you can only influence the first few steps. The rest the steps ahead are inevitable, and no matter how carefully you try to redirect the path, the future has a way of unfolding, even when you think you can alter the course.

When faced with choices, people often gravitate toward what feels less ordinary, something more exciting. It's not that Lucas was a "bad boy," but there was an undeniable pull to him that matched Laura's explorative personality. She grew up around her dad, the good guy—always doing things right with grace and poise. Jake, in many ways, reminded her of her dad. You'd think she would lean more toward him, but people crave variety, and Laura was no different. She was drawn to something a little different, a bit more thrilling.

Throughout their high school years, the once-stable triangle of friendship was shifting into something far more complicated: a love triangle. The longest side of the triangle was, of course, jealousy, with the other two sides weaving a delicate balance of love and resentment. As the natural leader of the group, Laura had the ability to navigate the awkwardness of being both a friend and a girlfriend to Lucas, while also keeping the strong bond with Jake. Jake, for his part, did most of the work, constantly proving he wasn't the third wheel. He worked hard to show that he could still be involved, helping maintain a sense of normalcy and avoiding any awkwardness. Yet, he also knew when to step back, understanding the importance of giving the couple space and respecting the balance of their evolving relationship.

The high school years drifted by, each day more about enjoying time with friends than focusing on the lessons that were supposed to be learned. Seeing familiar faces and the predictable rhythm of life made waking up each day an adventure of anticipation. The tasks of the day—small and simple—made time pass easily, with mental checkmarks marking their completion. The beginning of the day felt heavy, but as time ticked by, the weight lifted, replaced by a sense of accomplishment and the comfort of relaxation. After a full day, as the night took over, there was a quiet recharge, ready to face the next day.

This comfortable pattern came to a grinding halt when Laura's dad suffered a sudden heart attack. The loss of him was more than a shock it wasn't the kind of jolt that knocks the wind out of you; it was more like a slow, mournful feeling, like moving through molasses, disconnected and numb. It was her senior year, and with her sisters away at college, only she and her mom were left at home. The triangle of her parents' love was suddenly gone, leaving her feeling the urge to distance herself from the other triangle in her life the one between herself, Lucas, and Jake.

Her energy drained away, and she craved only simplicity no complications—letting life pass her by as time moved forward, whether she acknowledged it or not. It took a long time for her to talk to anyone again. She and Lucas silently agreed to return to their stable friendship, as though the boyfriend-girlfriend phase had never existed, a change so seamless that neither noticed it had ever been more.

In the midst of her immense grief, as if an invisible part of herself had been taken, Laura found herself drawn to the person who reminded her most of her father—Jake. He was there for her, offering comfort, like a teammate substituting in for a missing player. Jake and Lucas got along fine, even with the underlying tension, as they both became the most important men in Laura's life now that her father was gone. Their triangle remained, though the sides were unequal, yet it was stronger than any perfectly symmetrical shape. The things unseen in life—like invisible forces of nature are sometimes stronger than they seem, even ghostlike, but real. That was enough for Laura, Jake, and Lucas for now.

"Want me to get you the usual latte?" Peter asked, breaking her from her thoughts.

"Yeah, that's fine," Laura replied, still lost in the haze of her memories.

Laura's mind struggled to figure out where to start in telling Peter about her past. She knew it would help him understand the killer better, but more importantly, it would give him insight into who she really was. She liked being friends with both Peter and Adam, but she had never fully opened up about the drama with the men in her past. Kissing and telling wasn't something she believed in, unless it was with her close girlfriends. Now, with her new guy friends in Houston, she kept things light, focusing on general life conversations, avoiding any deep dives into her past emotional experiences.

"Peter, I have something to tell you," Laura said, gathering her thoughts. "You already know that I know the killer."

"Yeah, I know he's your ex, but no details," Peter interrupted, laughing. "By the way, I don't need any details," he added, trying to lighten the mood.

"David was my ex, but I want to talk about two of the men he killed first," Laura continued, picking up where she had left off. "The first man was named Jake, and the last one was Lucas. We were all friends growing up in Baton Rouge, from elementary school through high school. What makes it more complicated is that at different times, I was their girlfriend too."

"That's not too unusual, but it can be hard to navigate," Peter responded. "I mean, I had friends growing up who ended up dating within the group. It's natural when you spend so much time together and develop emotions."

"I was with Lucas first," Laura explained. "I had this extra attraction to him. But then, during my senior year of high school, my dad suddenly died of a heart attack. My whole world crashed, and I shut everything out for a while."

"I'm sorry, Laura, for your loss," Peter said sympathetically. "That must have been really tough, especially during your senior year. At least you had Lucas, Jake, your mom, and your sisters for support."

"It was okay," Laura replied, looking down. "But I just wanted to be left alone. I was closer to my dad than my mom, so it hurt a lot. Lucas tried his best, but I shut him out, and we stopped being close in a boyfriend-girlfriend way. After a while, Jake, Lucas, and I went back to being regular friends, but there was this hole inside me from losing my dad. I don't know how it happened, but I started to see a lot of my dad in Jake. And with that, I began to develop feelings for him. So, I started dating Jake."

"You had a lot going on," Peter said, his tone gentle. "How did you manage all of that? And then getting back into a relationship with Jake? How did Lucas handle the change?"

"Jake and Lucas were fine with it. It didn't really change things that much," Laura explained. "Boys are often more relaxed about relationships, especially when the group is made up of friends. I started to feel better, too, when I was seeing Jake as more than a friend. It felt comfortable, and I really needed the kindness Jake gave me."

"Okay, so you've dated three people related to this killing spree," Peter said. "Not sure how that helps us find where Adam is being held by the killer, but it's kind of crazy that the police haven't contacted you yet. Guess the detectives, including me, aren't very good at their jobs. It must be a record though, knowing and having relationships with most of the people involved in these murders." Peter laughed nervously, still trying to find a light side to everything that had happened.

It's easy to wonder if we somehow caused others' lives to take the twists and turns they did, both the bad and the good. We tend to focus on the bad outcomes, thinking that no matter how hard someone tries to do the right thing, bad things always pile up, leaving only the expectation of a tough life ahead. Did I mess up Jake so badly that he could never recover? Lucas was fine—just a little too ambitious, like his father, always reaching for what he thought was glory and purpose. But Jake was too gentle, too vulnerable for this world. His personality was likely set from birth, just as Lucas's was—to hunger for attention and typical societal rewards.

"Well, once high school was over and we went off to our different universities, we just drifted apart," Laura said. "It wasn't a fight or a goodbye—more like we walked away, and nothing ever really happened. You'd think there would've been a bad breakup or something, but there wasn't. We spent time together one moment, and then a few months later, we just stopped talking, and there wasn't really a reason to start the conversation again. In my life, I've accepted that people come and go. They were there for that one moment, and once that moment was over, it was done. Live as you can, as long as you can."

"I hope Adam is doing that now!" Peter exclaimed. "He needs to find a way to keep fighting until we find him."

"You think we can find him?" Laura asked.

"I don't know exactly how, but I have to believe we will," Peter answered. "I need to channel my father's side of the family. The men were good sheriffs—smart and brave—and they always found ways to overcome the bad. There's good in this world, and where there's good, there's always bad. And the other way around—when there's only bad, somehow good comes along. We need to focus on the good and help our friend. So, what's the story with you and your ex, David?"

Where was I to begin with David? He was complicated—that's what drew me to him. By the time I met him at LSU, he had already traveled the world, checking off sights most people only dream of seeing. At first, like any relationship, everything seemed perfect. But over time, the cracks appeared. With David, those cracks weren't just flaws; they were signs of something deeper, something dangerous lurking beneath the surface.

Laura gathered her thoughts. "David and I met in college at LSU. It was my junior year, and he had just enrolled. He was older than me four years, actually but he hadn't gone straight to college after high school. Instead, he traveled. His family had money, and they never pressured him to make real decisions about his life."

"We met playing in an intramural ultimate frisbee league. He told me he noticed me first—said he admired how I could take a fall and get right back up, bruises and all. He liked women who weren't fragile, who didn't conform to traditional expectations. We ended up together for the last two years of my time at LSU."

She hesitated, then continued. "When you're nearing the end of one phase of life and stepping into another, you either grow closer to the people around you or drift apart. I had a pattern of leaving people behind first Jake, then Lucas. When I told David about them, he became fixated on the idea. He wasn't used to being left behind. If anything, he was the one who decided when relationships ended. In that way, we were alike. But sensing change ahead, I instinctively started distancing myself."

Laura frowned, recalling an unsettling detail. "Now that I look back, David never talked much about his travels. Most people who've seen the world love sharing stories, but he didn't. Sometimes, I'd catch him scanning foreign newspapers always the crime sections and obituaries."

Peter's expression darkened. "That's not normal. If he's a serial killer now, maybe this isn't his first time."

"I asked him once why he was so obsessed with crime reports. He laughed it off, said he liked true crime, like those podcasts everyone listens to. But he had this way of talking about it, like he believed everyone had a dark side. He thought people weren't born good or bad—just opportunistic. If they could suppress empathy, they'd do whatever suited them. He said most people would choose to be bad if they knew they could get away with it."

Peter's jaw tightened. "You think he killed before?"

Laura swallowed hard. "I don't know. But now, I wonder if he was looking through those papers to see if the authorities had found his victims."

Peter exhaled sharply. "That would explain why he's more reckless now. Maybe those kills weren't enough. Maybe he needs to be noticed. He wants the world to see him—the way he thinks only a true serial killer should be seen."

A weight settled on Laura's chest. "Am I a curse to the men in my life?" she whispered.

Peter blinked. "What? Why would you say that?"

"Look at them," she said, voice thick with emotion. "My dad died suddenly, so young. Then Jake. Then Lucas. And now Adam… maybe he's next. Maybe you should stay away from me."

Peter leaned forward, his voice firm. "Laura, stop. Your dad's death wasn't your fault—it was just awful luck. And you aren't responsible for what David did to Jake and Lucas. The only one to blame is David. He's got this twisted 'Superman Complex.' He sees problems in the world and decides to 'fix' them, not by helping people, but by proving he can do whatever he wants without consequences. He thinks he's above cause and effect. But we can't let him win. We have to focus."

Laura took a shaky breath. "You're right. So… what do we do next?"

Peter's tone shifted to sharp determination. "In detective work, the first step is narrowing down where the criminal might be. We look at where he's killed before. If we're lucky, that's also where he's hiding."

"There are only two locations where he killed in Houston, and they're far apart," Laura said, tension lacing her voice.

"Yes," Peter nodded. "Bellaire Chinatown's Diho Square and the JP Morgan Chase building's Sky Lobby downtown. We need a third point to form a perimeter, something that might narrow down where he's operating from."

Laura's brow furrowed. "What about his phone? If we can track it, we might get his exact location."

Peter shook his head. "I don't trust that phone. David's too careful to let us track him that easily. But check where it is anyway."

Laura tapped at her screen, frowning. "That's weird. It's still in the same place we first saw it Hermann Park."

"Exactly what I expected," Peter muttered. "It's probably a burner or an old phone he left behind to throw us off. But even if it's a decoy, it might still tell us something. Let's head there."

As he drove toward Hermann Park, Peter's mind raced through the evidence, trying to connect the dots. He hated this—the feeling of being one step behind, of reacting instead of predicting. The best detectives didn't just follow clues; they anticipated the next move. But David wasn't making it easy. Every piece of evidence felt like a carefully placed breadcrumb leading nowhere.

Adam was depending on him. He had studied cases like this for years, but theory wasn't helping him now.

His thoughts drifted to his time in Los Angeles, to his old partner, Lisa Gonzalez. She had a way of breaking down a case, seeing the patterns others missed. They had cracked cases that felt unsolvable, pulling threads until something gave way. Maybe that's what he needed to do now—stop looking at where David had been and start thinking about where he was going next.

Peter gripped the wheel tighter as Hermann Park came into view. He glanced at Laura. "If David left that phone behind, he wanted us to find it. The question is—why?"

When Lisa and I first partnered up, we teased each other constantly, pretending to be oblivious to the places we called home. She grew up in Glendale, just north of downtown, while I was raised in Culver City, west of the city center. The two neighborhoods were barely twenty miles apart, yet to anyone from either side, it might as well have been two thousand—or the distance to New York City.

Lisa called me "hippy" because Culver City was close to Venice Beach, a place she saw as overrun with "weirdos" spreading eccentric beliefs to the naive. I, in turn, dubbed her "Walmart" since Glendale, to me, was just another endless stretch of concrete suburbia on the outskirts of Los Angeles. Like all the exaggerated nicknames we slapped onto friends, they were meant to amuse, not offend.

I had buried certain emotions deep, holding them back like a dam straining to contain a flood. It didn't help that Lisa and I had gone from work partners to something more—colleagues to friends, friends to lovers. The work we did was intense, and our hidden relationship only added another layer of pressure. Every day, we faced the possibility of death on the job, yet we had to conceal what we truly meant to each other from our unit. You'd think having someone to share your fears with would ease the weight of it all. And for brief moments, it did. But reality always pulled us back, forcing us to confront the impossible task of stopping pain and suffering in the world while, inevitably, inflicting harm on each other.

I wasn't sure why, of all times, the past was creeping in now. I had been good at blocking it out, keeping it from tangling me in regret and guilt. But sometimes, I had to let the feelings come to course through me and empty out in an overwhelming surge, only to fade briefly before returning again.

Lisa and I had been assigned to investigate the recent deaths of Latino teenagers near Venice Beach. On the surface, they looked like drug overdoses, but we had to follow every lead, tracing the evidence back to its source. Our job meant talking to people who knew the streets and hoping that the information they shared sometimes willingly, sometimes not led us to something real.

Los Angeles had everything. It wasn't just a city; it was a patchwork of contradictions. Parks sprawled across the landscape beach parks, grassy parks, hiking trails that wound through the hills. Yet, for all its life, L.A. shouldn't exist the way it does. It only became what it is by siphoning water from distant mountains long ago. Water, more precious than any metal, sustained over four million people living in what was, at its core, a desert disguised as an oasis.

The character of a city, I often thought, was shaped by its sprawl, by the width and breadth of its reach. Some would argue that flat, sprawling cities were monotonous, repeating the same street corner over and over, forcing you to hunt for the hidden gems buried in the vastness. Others believed that densely stacked places like New York made every square foot count, filling every inch with life. But somehow, Los Angeles managed to be both. It stretched endlessly, yet it never felt empty. You could spend a lifetime exploring, finding something new, even in places you thought you'd already seen.

Venice Beach was truly a place like no other—perfect for walking, watching people, and immersing yourself in a world that felt like it followed its own unwritten rules. It was as if, long ago, someone had decreed that every oddity, every eccentric soul, every slice of life in Los Angeles should be drawn into this tiny stretch of sand and cement.

Lisa and I faced an immediate challenge in our investigation: getting people to talk. In Venice, unless you blended into the subcultures that lined the beach, you were just another outsider.

And there were plenty of groups—the bodybuilders at Muscle Beach, the volleyball players, the surfers, the skateboarders, the tourists, the pickleball fanatics, and the drifters who had made the boardwalk their home.

At least the teenage deaths had occurred in the same general area—the Venice Breakwater outlook. The bodies were always left there between three and five a.m. on either a Tuesday or Thursday. Whether these kids had overdosed or been deliberately targeted, we didn't know. But it was strange—always the same location, always the same nights. It was as if someone was collecting these teens off the streets, using them for something, and then discarding them like trash once they were no longer needed.

Another troubling piece of evidence: no families had come forward to claim the bodies. That suggested the victims weren't local. They had come from outside Los Angeles—perhaps lured, perhaps taken, but ultimately abandoned here.

With the little evidence we had, Lisa and I decided to stake out the drop site on the next Tuesday and Wednesday, watching for anything unusual. Since my apartment was near Venice Beach, I told Lisa to stay over instead of meeting up. It was an easy cover—detective partners working late together wouldn't raise suspicion. But people love to speculate, and when a man and a woman spend enough time in each other's company, assumptions always follow.

Most moments in life pass unnoticed—harmless, routine, forgettable. Until something goes wrong. Then, those same moments become haunting, irreversible. A split-second miscalculation, a decision made too soon or too late, and everything changes.

I wasn't with Lisa that night. I wasn't her official boyfriend, so I hadn't gone to dinner with her at her parents' house. She had been tired and decided to stay overnight, setting an alarm so she could leave early and meet me before our stakeout.

At two a.m., she texted me to say she was on her way. Instead of coming straight to my place, she took a detour past Venice Beach—it was on the way, and maybe she had a gut feeling that something would be different this time. It had been three weeks since the last body was found, breaking the pattern of four consecutive weeks of deaths.

Then Lisa saw the van.

The kind of van that didn't belong. No windows. The kind you only see in movies, the kind that makes your stomach tighten in instinctive warning.

She slowed her car, watching it. She texted me to come. Now.

I barely remember moving. One moment, I was in my apartment; the next, I was on the road, my heart hammering. I don't recall grabbing my keys, opening the door, or even how I drove just the raw urgency, the way my pulse pounded louder than the engine. I reached Venice Beach in under five minutes. It felt like an hour.

And then everything was already over.

Things that should take hours had unraveled in minutes, altering everything. Freezing what was once warm.

Lisa's car was there, angled awkwardly, its right front tire mounted over the jagged curb. Smoke curled from the crumpled metal of the hood, its once-smooth surface twisted like a crushed bedsheet. The car had slammed into one of the heavy iron poles that lined the sidewalk, the kind linked together with thick, sinewy chains.

The passenger door hung open. It had scraped against the pavement, leaving a deep, pale scar in the concrete.

Lisa was nowhere to be seen.

I jumped out of my car, leaving it in the middle of the street beside Lisa's abandoned vehicle. My gun was already in my hand, ripped from its holster, my mind ready to unload every last round into whoever had taken her. At that moment, I wasn't a detective. I wasn't bound by the law. I was pure rage, a man ready to kill for the woman he loved.

I reached the open car door, heart pounding, but Lisa wasn't there. No sign of a struggle. No sign of her at all.

Then I turned to my right—toward the Venice Breakwater outlook.

I ran, praying that when I got there, I would find nothing. That Lisa would text me any second to say she had lost the van, that she was fine. That this was just another bad lead.

But then I saw them.

Four bodies, piled up. Three young Latino teenagers stacked in a pyramid, and beneath them—Lisa.

Her eyes were open. A bullet hole marked the center of her forehead.

I tore through the bodies, throwing them aside like they were nothing. My hands shook as I pulled Lisa onto my lap, cradling her, my breath coming in broken, gasping sobs.

"No. No. No. No. No. No." The word spilled out of me, over and over, meaningless and desperate.

Her eyes still open stared past me, their glassy surface catching the dim light like curved, translucent windows. But they saw nothing. Would never see anything again. No more light. No more touch, sound, scent, or taste.

She was gone.

I shut her eyes for the last time. I pressed my lips to her forehead, her cheek, her lips—one final goodbye.

And then, something inside me collapsed. A deep, endless hole opened up, swallowing me whole, suffocating everything I was.

Only one thought cut through the darkness.

I would find them. I would kill them.

I wasn't a detective anymore. I wasn't going to wait for courts, for justice, for answers. Lisa was my world, and they had destroyed it. Now, I would destroy them.

I made it back to my car, barely registering anything around me. My vision tunneled, my only thought fixed on that van, somewhere in the streets of Los Angeles. I drove like a man possessed, shifting manically between lanes, though the roads were empty at four a.m. My hands clenched the wheel, white-knuckled, heart hammering with a singular purpose.

I called the department. My voice was steady, empty. "My partner is dead. Three other teenagers too."

Then I drove. For two hours, I searched. Nothing. The van had vanished again, just like before.

By the time I was called back to the precinct, I had nothing but rage left in me.

Chief Reed Ayers was waiting, his expression unreadable. I sat across from him, recounting every detail—what Lisa and I had planned, how she had decided to drive by Venice Beach first, how everything had gone wrong in a matter of minutes.

Then he leveled his gaze at me and asked the one question that cut deeper than any bullet ever could.

"I'm going to ask this straight, and don't play dumb with me," he said. "Did your relationship with Lisa fuck this up and get her killed?"

Reed's accusation blindsided me. How the hell did he know? Lisa and I had kept our relationship quiet—careful. Or at least, I thought we had. Maybe it wasn't as much of a secret as I believed. Maybe Reed was just throwing bait into the water, hoping I'd bite.

"What are you talking about, Reed?" I snapped. "How do you know? Does the whole department know?"

Reed leaned back, studying me with that unreadable expression of his. "I don't know if everyone here does, but I do. I have a good hunch for these things," he said evenly. "Besides, I've been down that road before—getting involved with my partner. It messes with your judgment."

"Our relationship didn't get her killed," I said, my voice hard. "She saw the van. She didn't want them getting away. She called me. I was just too late."

Reed sighed, shaking his head. "Peter, you're off this case. You need to take a step back."

"Reed, I want this case," I shot back. "You have to let me see it through."

"No," he said firmly. "And you're dismissed."

Just like that.

The van disappeared. The killers were never found. The case remained open, but it might as well have been dead. And just like that, the bodies stopped appearing at Venice Beach. The last time three teenagers were dumped was the last time Lisa took a breath in this world.

That was when I learned—good doesn't always win. Sometimes, bad gets ahead. Maybe most of the time. Or maybe it's just a coin flip—half and half, chance deciding which side gets to live.

I couldn't stay after that. I started looking for other jobs—anything, anywhere. Even considered heading back to Bishop, where my extended family still lived. I wanted to disappear, to get away from the streets that carried memories like ghosts. Every block, every turn, every flashing neon sign held a moment of Lisa and me, frozen in time.

That's the thing about memory. It doesn't belong to the past. It replays like a film stuck on loop, making everything feel like it's still happening. The past isn't the past to the brain. The past is the present.

And when I felt trapped in that endless cycle of pain, a job posting from Houston caught my eye. They were looking for detectives.

I applied. I hoped.

The call came, and I took it.

That's how I ended up in Houston.

"Everything okay, Peter?" Laura asked, watching him closely.

"Yeah, just thinking back on my life before coming here," Peter said, shaking his head slightly. "Sorry, I got caught up in my thoughts."

"No, it's fine," Laura assured him. "Just wanted to check in and see what our next move is. I'm a little blank at the moment."

"Me too," Peter admitted, but his voice carried determination. "But we'll get through this together. I had a partner in Los Angeles. We were close—really close. We got separated during an investigation, and she was killed. I won't let that happen again. You and Adam mean too much to me. We're going to catch David. Nothing bad is going to happen to you, and we will save Adam."

Laura reached over, touching Peter's hand with a warmth that went beyond simple reassurance. It wasn't just a gesture of support or quiet understanding it was something more. A crossing of an invisible line, one that friends often build early in their relationship. And Peter felt it, recognizing the silent shift between them. His fingers instinctively relaxed, responding to the unspoken message between them.

They had been to Hermann Park countless times—sometimes with Adam, sometimes alone. Now, as Peter pulled into the parking lot, he couldn't shake the weight of déjà vu pressing down on him. Another public park. Another chase. Another moment where someone he cared about was in danger. He took a deep breath, steadying himself. Step by step. Don't get ahead of yourself.

"Let's go find that phone," Peter said as he got out of the car, Laura right behind him.

"Okay, looks like we're about six hundred feet from where the phone should be," Laura said, checking her screen. "But why do we need it if we already know it's a fake? It's not his real phone."

"I want to see if we can get inside," Peter explained. "There's a chance he messed up—left something behind that we can use to track him."

"And how exactly do we get in?" Laura asked.

Peter smirked. "That's where I'm hoping you can help. You were his girlfriend—maybe you remember his passcode?"

Laura frowned, digging through her memories, scanning for numbers David had used—Wi-Fi passwords, app purchases, security codes. Then she remembered.

"3142," she said suddenly.

Peter raised an eyebrow. "You're sure?"

"Pretty sure," Laura nodded. "He liked '314' because of the mathematical value of pi, and he tacked on the '2' because it fit into the common '1234' sequence in a way that was easy to remember. He used it all the time."

They picked up their pace, weaving through Hermann Park. If they had been in running gear, they would have blended in perfectly with the other joggers, but neither of them cared about the eyes trailing them. Their focus was locked on one thing.

"Where's the dot now?" Peter asked.

"We're right on top of it," Laura said, glancing at her phone. "The phone should be around here somewhere."

Peter took a moment to catch his breath, scanning their surroundings. They had stopped at the entrance of the McGovern Centennial Gardens. As they stepped inside, their eyes were immediately drawn to The Mount, a thirty-foot-high earth mound at the far end of the gardens. It blended seamlessly into the landscape, with spiraling shrub-lined paths leading up to an observation deck overlooking Hermann Park.

"I bet David's burner phone is up there somewhere," Peter muttered.

Laura sighed. "That's like finding a needle in a haystack."

Peter smirked. "Let's just hope those bushes don't fight back too much. We're going to have to go through them one by one. People are going to think we're insane."

Laura chuckled. "We'll just smile and say we're on an adult scavenger hunt. Maybe geocaching."

They climbed The Mount, checking every bush, turning over dirt, searching every possible hiding spot. By the time they reached the top, their hands were scratched and dirt-covered, their minds drained. They collapsed onto a bench at the peak, staring blankly over Hermann Park.

Laura checked her phone again. The blue tracking dot for David's burner phone hadn't moved. In fact, their own GPS marker was directly on top of it. If this were darts, they would have hit a perfect bullseye.

Peter exhaled slowly. Despite the exhaustion, despite the weight of everything hanging over them, there was a strange kind of peace in sitting there with Laura.

All over the world, people were fighting their own battles—millions, maybe billions, trying to claw their way toward some kind of peace. They were the real warriors, the unseen heroes, those who carried their struggles in silence, forcing their broken minds to believe in hope. Because what other choice was there? The only option left to the surviving spirit was to keep going.

"Live as you can, as long as you can."

Laura's words echoed in Peter's mind just as a vibration buzzed against his palm. A new text appeared on their screens, sending a cold shiver through them both.

"Two blind mice looking and looking for David and Adam!"

Peter stiffened. Laura's phone screen glowed with the same message.

"How the hell does he do that?" Peter muttered, his jaw tightening. "How does he always know? He must be here, watching us seeing us scramble up this mound like fools, chasing a phone he isn't even using."

"I told you he has hobbies," Laura muttered. "Ones that are nefarious and cunningly lethal. And now, we're just guinea pigs—chasing his twisted game while he watches."

Another text from David appeared.

'Okay, I will help you,' it read. 'You are sitting on it!'

"We're sitting on it!" Laura blurted out, eyes wide.

Peter's gaze dropped to the bench beneath them—one of those familiar marble park benches found in green spaces across the world. The kind carved from fossilized stone, where ancient marine shells had once left behind their ghostly imprints, dissolved by acidic waters millions of years ago.

He ran his hand under the bench, fingers gliding along the smooth, cold underside. Tilting his head to see where his touch was leading, his breath caught.

A phone.

Duct-taped to the center, flush against the marble.

The next text came instantly.

'Happy to help,' David wrote. 'And yes, Laura is right. The passcode is 3142. Two blind mice are doing well so far by keeping the police and your detective buddies, Peter, out of this. Keep it that way… or I might do something stupid. And start harming. Maybe even killing. Your Adam. Yes, Adam is still with us. And as long as you two blind mice stay blind, for now, he stays alive.'

A heavy silence hung between them.

"What do we do now?" Laura asked, her voice edged with urgency.

Peter didn't hesitate.

"We open this damn phone and see if there's anything in here that gets us closer to Adam!" he said, tapping in 3142.

Die When You Can

"I just texted your friends," David said, calm as ever, like it was just another everyday conversation.

"You texted Peter and Laura?" I asked, my confusion sharp and immediate.

"Yeah, I got bored with you," David laughed. "Kidding just the boring parts of you. But I did text them. Looks like they're at Hermann Park, on a date. No longer blind mice, now lovebirds. Again, I tease. What I mean is, they were looking for my other phone, and I helped them find it. Now, they can move along the gameboard."

"This is a game to you?" I snapped. "What did they what did I do to deserve this? How do you justify murder?"

"I'm not justifying anything, Adam," David said, still unnervingly composed. "I never claimed I was right or that what I do is good. I know I'm wrong by society's rules, at least. But I stopped believing in those rules long ago, even before New Orleans. Before Houston.

"Morality? It's just another construct, a distraction to keep people from realizing the truth. Rules exist to pacify overthinking minds, to create order for those who would otherwise tear each other apart. But at its core, the world isn't about fairness it's about control. A few people make the decisions, the rest of us obey. That's the real game.

"I'll never be one of those few. I'll never shape laws or dictate who rises and who falls. But I can carve out my own space my own set of rules. I can move people like you, like them, across the board. I can play God in my own way."

The more David talked, the clearer it became he wasn't just another lunatic with delusions of grandeur. He was meticulous, strategic. Every detail had been planned, every move anticipated. He wasn't just playing a game; he was controlling it. Peter and Laura were being guided closer and closer, but David wouldn't allow that unless he was absolutely certain of his position. His confidence wasn't arrogance it was the certainty of a man who believed he had already accounted for every possible outcome. That terrified me more than anything. He had woven an intricate web, and we were all tangled in it, moving exactly as he intended. I needed to start thinking ahead, preparing for the moment I would have to fight back. Because the way this was unfolding, that moment wasn't far away.

David, however, seemed unfazed, slipping into thought as if he were preparing for another lecture, another chance to unravel his philosophy for me. His past, his worldview—it was all leading somewhere. He wanted me to listen.

"History is nothing more than a distorted reflection in a shattered mirror," he finally said, his voice casual, almost indifferent. "From the moment civilization began—at least from the parts we were allowed to remember it has been shaped by the elite. A handful of people controlling the narrative, dictating what is true and what isn't, bending reality to fit their purpose. And the rest of us? We consume it, internalize it, pass it along as if it were fact. We don't even question it. The powerful get to write history, and the powerless become footnotes, erased or rewritten to fit the story being told."

I remained silent, but my mind was racing. His words were unsettling, not because they were entirely false, but because there was an uncomfortable degree of truth woven into them.

"You see, people love to convince themselves they understand the past," he continued. "Historians, intellectuals they dig through ruins, analyze bones, pore over ancient texts, trying to reconstruct what life was like thousands of years ago. But it's a fool's game. They'll never truly know. They base their assumptions on fragments, on biased accounts passed down through time, on a present-day lens that distorts everything. The past is always incomplete, shaped by those who controlled it then and reinterpreted by those who control it now. The only thing that has remained unchanged, the only real constant, is power. The rich dictated history then, and they dictate it now. The rest are just spectators, filling in the blanks with whatever makes them feel less insignificant."

His gaze drifted as he spoke, as if lost in thought, but I could sense it the need to be heard, to be remembered. He wasn't just sharing a viewpoint; he was inserting himself into the long lineage of those who had shaped narratives before him. He was another self-important voice demanding to be acknowledged. Another person desperate to carve his name into something larger than himself. And now, it was time for David's Storytime again.

"The world is black and white when you travel," he said, shifting gears with a slow, deliberate exhale. "No shades of gray, no blurred lines, no moral ambiguity. Right and wrong are dictated by who holds the upper hand. The one taking controls the game, and the one losing has no say in it. Cambodia taught me that. There, a single word dominates everything Dollar. And not just any dollar. The U.S. dollar. It doesn't matter where you go, what language they speak, or how deep their struggle's run money is the only universal truth.

"I'll never forget the first time I saw it. A child standing on the streets of Siem Reap, barefoot, wearing a tattered shirt, her ribs visible beneath thin skin. And around her neck? A massive boa constrictor, lazily coiled like a scarf. It should have been absurd, surreal even, but it wasn't. It was calculated. She wasn't afraid of the snake, and neither was I. But she knew the effect it would have on tourists. She knew how to make them stop, hesitate, pull out their wallets. And all the while, she repeated it 'Picture one dollar, picture one dollar, picture one dollar.' Over and over, like a hypnotic chant. She had learned, at an age when she should have been playing with dolls, that survival had nothing to do with fairness or innocence. It was about leverage. About knowing how to make someone part with their money."

David fell silent for a moment, as if letting his words settle. Then, with a slight smirk, he added, "And you wonder why I stopped believing in morality."

Most travelers come to Siem Reap to witness the grandeur of Angkor Wat, the heart of an ancient civilization that once thrived in the dense jungles of Cambodia. Scattered across the Angkor region are thousands of structures, built nearly a thousand years ago, their intricate carvings and towering spires standing as a testament to human ambition and artistry. But nature, relentless and indifferent, has woven itself into these ruins massive tree roots twist through cracks in the stone, branches stretch skyward, assimilating with the temples as if reclaiming what was once its own. People are drawn here by the images they've seen the dreamlike silhouettes of temples at sunrise, the remnants of a lost empire calling them to walk through history, to glimpse a world long past.

Yet, for all its ancient wonders, Cambodia's more recent history is just as compelling though far bloodier. The last fifty years alone have been defined by upheaval, a relentless cycle of conflict and devastation. In 1970, while Prince Norodom Sihanouk was abroad, he unknowingly lost his country. A coup, led by Prime Minister Lon Nol, reshaped Cambodia overnight, plunging it into a five-year civil war. As with most political struggles, two factions emerged, neither willing to compromise, both determined to spill blood over their ideologies. Foreign powers—China,

Vietnam, the U.S., and others intervened, but their presence only deepened the chaos rather than resolving it. Between 1970 and 1975, Cambodia became another battlefield in a larger geopolitical game, a nation torn apart by forces far beyond its borders.

Then came the Khmer Rouge. Led by Pol Pot, they didn't just seize control they finalized it. What followed from 1975 to 1979 was nothing short of genocide, a nightmarish campaign of extermination that left the country in ruins. The scars of that era remain not just in history books, but in the faces of those who survived, in the unspoken grief that lingers in the air, in the struggles that persist decades later.

How much damage can a single decade inflict? Enough to shatter a nation, to warp its trajectory for generations. Even today, the echoes of that violent past ripple through Cambodia's streets. A ten-year-old girl stands barefoot in Siem Reap, a snake coiled around her shoulders, its length extending past her small frame. She isn't afraid of it this is her livelihood, her way of surviving in a world that has never been fair. Her voice is repetitive, rhythmic, almost mechanical: "Picture one dollar, picture one dollar, picture one dollar." A transaction as simple as it is tragic.

Maybe Cambodia was always like this fractured, struggling, fighting against forces beyond its control. But that isn't unique. Every country, every civilization, has its own stories of destruction, of people divided by power, of morality twisted to justify war. Conflict always comes in two parts two sides, each believing itself righteous, each labeling the other as the villain. The world craves simple narratives, clean distinctions of good and evil. But history is never that simple.

Something was waking up inside me. I couldn't quite define it an unease, a shift, like something dormant stirring, yet not fully formed. I sat with it, moving in a confused state, unsure whether it was excitement, curiosity, or something else entirely.

Then, as if the universe sensed my restlessness, a young Cambodian man approached me, offering to drive me anywhere I wanted for just twenty-five dollars. It was an absurdly low price. In most cities, twenty-five dollars wouldn't even get you a ten-minute Uber ride, yet here was a man his name was Borai Sok offering himself and his car for the entire day. I didn't hesitate. I accepted.

Borai drove me through the vast ruins of Angkor Wat, taking me beyond the well-trodden paths, deep into the forests where forgotten temples stood in quiet defiance of time. The grandeur of the past pressed in from all sides intricate carvings whispering of civilizations long gone, stone corridors swallowed by roots of ancient trees. Beyond the temples, we ventured to the floating villages of Tonle Sap Lake, the largest freshwater lake in Southeast Asia. I watched as families lived out their lives in wooden houses bobbing gently on the water, their entire existence dictated by the lake's rise and fall. We stopped at an Angkor silk farm, where I saw firsthand the meticulous process of silk-making delicate worms fed on mulberry leaves before being boiled to extract their silk, their short lives sacrificed for fabric that would one day drape across foreign bodies in faraway places.

With Borai, I wasn't just sightseeing I was absorbing the rhythm of Cambodia itself, the beauty in its raw, unfiltered existence. I had seen so much in one day that I didn't want it to end.

"Borai, I'd like to hire you for another day," I said, feeling the pull to keep going.

He hesitated. "But sir, I have shown you all that I know. There is nothing left in Siem Reap." His voice was direct, honest.

"Then take me somewhere unexpected," I replied. "Show me something that's not in the guidebooks. Surprise me. I'll be happy just to have your company and see whatever you think is worth seeing."

Borai considered this for a moment, then nodded. "Fine, sir. I will pick you up outside your hotel tomorrow morning at 9 a.m."

"Sounds good. See you then."

But moments have a way of shifting everything of grabbing you when you least expect it and steering you toward something irreversible.

That night, restless in my hotel room, I decided to wander Siem Reap's main street, letting the city's pulse guide me. It was night market time a chaotic, intoxicating mix of sound, scent, and movement. People wove through narrow stalls, bartering over cheap clothing, handcrafted jewelry, and figurines of strange, forgotten gods. The air carried the mingling aromas of grilled meats, tropical fruits, and the sharp tang of spices. I sipped an ice-cold one-dollar beer, letting the bitterness settle on my tongue, while a vendor handed me five-dollar pork cooked in pumpkin curry, spread generously over rice. The richness of the meal, the warmth of the humid air against my skin, the hum of foreign voices around me it was everything a traveler long for.

For the first time in a long time, I felt completely untethered. Alone, yet not lonely. A stranger in a foreign land, but content in the simplest way imaginable.

As I decided to head back to my hotel, I was confronted by another foreigner someone who, like me, wasn't a local. At first, I assumed he was just another traveler looking to strike up a casual conversation. He asked where I was from, tossing out small talk like bait, hoping it would lead to something more interesting. His accent and mannerisms told me he was likely American, but I never got the chance to confirm. Before I could learn his name, his story, or even the reason for his presence in Cambodia, the situation shifted.

A switchblade flashed in his hand.

The ease with which he presented the weapon sent a sharp dose of adrenaline through me. My surroundings, once alive with the sounds of the night market, suddenly felt isolated. He motioned for me to move, leading me down a dimly lit alley behind the main street. The flickering lights overhead cast long, exaggerated cone-shaped shadows against the walls, stretching and distorting reality, creating the perfect cover for encounters like this covert, discreet, and all too common.

"So, what's on you that's about to be mine?" the stranger asked, his voice laced with excitement.

I kept my expression cold, measured. "I have some cash. Take it and leave me alone."

His gaze dropped to my chest. "That necklace looks expensive. I want that too."

"No," I said, my voice firm.

His demeanor shifted. "What do you mean, no?" he snapped. "You don't get it, do you? I have a knife. I'll cut you bad if you don't listen."

I met his glare without hesitation. "I'm not giving you my necklace," I said. "It was my father's. It means everything to me."

The stranger sneered. "I don't care about you, or your father."

And that's where he made his mistake.

He had no idea who he was dealing with no idea about my past, my training, or what I was capable of. He saw another unsuspecting tourist, an easy target. What he didn't see was the extensive fighting background my father had instilled in me from childhood. My father had taught me that intelligence and strength weren't separate forces; they were one and the same. The mind and body had to be trained equally, developed to their fullest potential.

He was never harsh with me, never a drill sergeant barking orders. Instead, he reasoned with me, guided me, placed me in situations where I could learn, where I could grow. And I did. I studied. I trained. I pushed myself. I learned how to read people their stances, their intentions, the moment before they made their move. I had been taught to be both the smartest and the bravest in any situation.

And now, I was about to put that training to use.

I pretended to comply, reaching behind my head as if to unfasten the latch on my necklace. My fingers brushed against the clasp, but my focus remained on the stranger the way he held the knife close to my stomach, the tension in his stance, the cocky glint in his eyes. He thought he was in control.

He wasn't.

In a sudden, fluid motion, I swung my right hand, striking him hard with the base of my palm the thick, fleshy part that delivered the most impact. The force of the hit startled him, sending him stumbling back a step, his grip on the knife loosening. Before he could regain his footing, I balled my left hand into a tight fist and drove it into his throat, landing a direct hit on his larynx. His breath hitched, his eyes widened in panic, and he crumpled forward, choking uncontrollably, gasping as his body fought for air.

The knife slipped from his fingers, clattering onto the pavement. He bent forward, hands clawing at his throat, still struggling to breathe.

I bent down, picked up the weapon, and turned it over in my hand. Now it was my turn to talk.

"Alright, first things first," I said, my voice steady. "What's your name?"

Between ragged breaths, he shot me a glare. "Why should I tell you?"

I twirled the knife in my fingers before tightening my grip. "Look, I'm trying to be civil here, have a polite conversation. And don't even think about running." I stepped closer. "You've already seen what I can do. If you so much as twitch, I could easily catch you and stab you in the back."

His eyes flickered with fear. Defeated, he exhaled. "Robert Stevens."

"Alright, Robert. Why did you try to rob me?" I studied him for a moment. "You don't exactly look like a guy who needs to steal."

He let out a dry chuckle. "I don't do it because I need to." His breathing was still shaky, but he seemed to be calming down. "I do it for fun."

I frowned. "Fun?"

"Yeah," Robert admitted, his tone shifting from fear to something closer to pride. "Every time I travel, on the last night before I fly home, I pick someone. It's a high I can't stop chasing."

"You're telling me you plan to steal from people on vacation? Every time?"

He nodded. "Started years ago. I was a bully as a kid treated people like shit. Then, on my first trip to Thailand, I tried it out. Just grabbed some guy, took his stuff, and walked away clean. It wasn't even about the money. It was the feeling. The control. That moment when someone realizes they're helpless that's what gets me."

I raised an eyebrow. "And you only steal from men?"

Robert scoffed. "Yeah. Women? No. Never. Wouldn't get the same rush. And besides, I don't want the stuff women carry. I take from men. I keep their things—trophies from my wins."

I let his words settle between us. "And before tonight, this always worked for you?"

"Yeah," he said.

"How many times?"

He hesitated, then shrugged. "About twenty."

I let out a low whistle. "Impressive record." A smirk tugged at the corner of my lips. "Well, tonight's your unlucky night. And there aren't going to be any more."

Robert's expression shifted. The bravado in his voice faded. "I know I was wrong," he stammered. "I won't do this anymore. I promise."

I tilted my head, watching him. "No, you won't," I said calmly. "Because I'm going to kill you. Here and now."

His body stiffened. He took a step back, his face draining of color. "Wait… what?" His voice cracked. "You're crazy." His gaze darted around the alley. "I— I'm out of here. I'm sorry, alright? I shouldn't have done this!" He turned abruptly, panic flooding his features. "I'm leaving now!"

As Robert turned to flee, I moved first. Leading with my left foot, I hooked it around his ankle, sending him crashing to the ground. Before he could react, I pressed my right hand against the back of his neck, forcing his face into the pavement, while my left hand pinned his lower back, keeping him immobilized.

I didn't hesitate. The knife was still in my grip. With swift, deliberate force, I drove the blade into his side once, twice, again and again, each strike sinking deep, each movement precise. His body convulsed beneath me, a gurgled gasp escaping his lips as his limbs twitched in useless protest. His struggle weakened with every stab, but I had no intention of leaving room for uncertainty. I shifted, adjusted my grip, and in one final motion, I plunged the knife into the side of his head, the blade slicing through skull and into brain matter. His body stiffened—and then, nothing.

I exhaled, steady, composed. There was no rush, no panic. Only purpose.

Moving quickly, I dragged his body toward a nearby dumpster, making sure to bury him beneath layers of trash concealing him at the very bottom, covering him with whatever refuse was already inside. The stench of rotting food and waste mixed with the coppery tang of blood, but it didn't faze me. I wiped the knife clean of any evidence, tucked it into my pocket, and walked away, slipping seamlessly back into the night.

By the time I reached my hotel, my heartbeat had slowed, my breathing even. I felt lighter, as if I had shed some invisible weight. I climbed into bed and, for the first time since my trip began, slept soundly deep, undisturbed, at peace.

The Next Morning

Right on time, at exactly 9 a.m., Borai arrived.

"Good morning, sir," he greeted, smiling as he stepped out of his car.

"Good morning, Borai," I replied, then added, "And please, you can just call me David."

"Yes, sir sorry, I mean David," he corrected himself with a small laugh.

I wasted no time. "I have a task today, if you don't mind," I said, my tone measured. "It's delicate, but I think with your attention to detail, you can help me. And I'd be willing to pay you one thousand U.S. dollars for your assistance."

Borai raised an eyebrow, chuckling. "That's a lot of money," he said. Then, with a half-smirk, he added jokingly, "What are we doing? Killing someone and getting rid of the body?"

I met his gaze, unflinching.

"Not quite," I said, calmly, directly, matter-of-fact. "I already killed the man last night. Now, we need to retrieve the body and dispose of it discreetly, efficiently. I trust you know a good place to discard it."

Borai's laughter faded. He went silent, his expression unreadable.

I opened the car door and got in. Without a word, he followed, started the engine, and pulled out onto the road.

We drove in silence.

As we reached the alley where Robert had met his end, Borai parked. He stepped out, opened the trunk, and waited. I walked over to the dumpster, grabbed Robert's lifeless body, and without hesitation, lifted him into the trunk, shutting it firmly.

It was time to finish the job.

"Okay, Borai, that man you just saw attacked me last night," I said, my voice calm, measured. "Unfortunately, I had no choice but to kill him I feared for my life."

Borai glanced at me through the rearview mirror, his expression tight, his grip on the wheel firm. "I understand, sir sorry, David," he corrected himself, his voice laced with unease.

I exhaled, shifting in my seat. "Before we get on with our day, do you know of any good places where we can dispose of the body?"

Borai hesitated only for a moment before nodding. "Yes. There's a place that locals know, where the ground is never disturbed. We can bury the body there, and it will never be found."

Something about his response made me pause. "Why there? Sounds like sacred ground. Should we even be touching it?"

"It's okay," Borai assured me. "It's a mass burial site—only a few of us know about it. It's the safest option."

A realization settled over me like a heavy shadow. "A mass killing site… left by the Khmer Rouge?" I asked, my voice quieter now.

Borai's hands tightened on the steering wheel. "Yes," he answered simply.

We drove the rest of the way in silence. The weight of what we were about to do pressed against my chest, but I said nothing. The trees thickened as we left the city limits, the paved roads giving way to dirt paths that twisted deeper into the forest. It felt like we had been driving for hours, though in reality, only twenty minutes had passed.

When the job was done, Borai suggested we return to his home to clean up and eat. I agreed.

At Borai's Home

His house sat at the end of a compacted mud-dirt driveway; the surface so solid it felt like driving over asphalt. A few trees lined the yard, casting enough shade to keep the small house cool despite the relentless heat. Beyond it stretched an open, sun-drenched backyard, where curry plants grew among patches of grass, and rice fields shimmered in still, watery ponds.

Inside, the air was thick with the scent of spices and earth. We drank ice-cold Coca-Colas straight from thick glass bottles the kind you only ever see in old advertisements and classic films. The first sip was sharp, refreshing against the humid weight of the day.

Borai's wife soon appeared, offering a warm smile as she introduced herself. She carried a tray of fresh fruit, warm flatbread, curry, and skewered meat seasoned with a mix of spices that filled the air with their aroma.

Inside the house, his elderly grandparents rested in the shade, seeking relief from the oppressive tropical heat. Outside, their three children—two boys and a girl—ran through the yard, chasing each other across the rice fields, their laughter carrying through the air. Rivers of sweat streamed down their small bodies, but they didn't seem to mind.

They were used to it.

"Here, my friend," I said, handing Borai one thousand U.S. dollars.

His eyes widened as he instinctively took a step back. "No, no, no, no!" he protested, shaking his head. "I can't take that much. You only hired my car for twenty-five dollars."

"Borai, please take it," I insisted, my tone firm yet sincere. "I told you I would pay you, and I'm not leaving until you accept it. Today was a lot of work, and I asked you to do some difficult things. You did nothing wrong you only helped me get rid of a bad person, someone who was trying to hurt me."

Borai hesitated, then, with a deep breath, took the money. "Thank you, David," he said quietly. "I will not forget your kindness."

I studied him for a moment before speaking again. "Some people must live by the idea 'Die when you can.' Do you know what I mean?"

Borai frowned. "Sorry, no I don't understand."

I leaned back, taking in the warm air of the Cambodian afternoon. "We don't know when we'll die," I explained. "So, live your life as if it could end at any moment. If you do that, you'll make sure to enjoy each day as fully as possible. If you truly embrace that, every day becomes your last day, and you'll make damn sure you live it right."

Borai smiled, nodding slightly. "Okay, sir sorry, David."

I smirked. "Well, I hope that guy I killed had a good last day before crossing my path." The words rolled off my tongue with amusement, the smirk lingering on my lips like an inside joke only I understood.

After finishing our food and drinks, I let Borai know I was tired and wanted to return to my hotel. My flight back to the States was the next day, and I needed rest before the long journey. As he pulled up to my hotel, I took a final glance at him, memorizing the face of the man who had shown me so much during my time in Cambodia a man who had unknowingly helped me step further into the person I was becoming.

Later That Night

Upstairs in my hotel room, I stretched out on the bed, the cool air from the vent washing over me. My body was still, but my mind raced.

Robert had been the first.

And now, I wanted more.

I had always had the skill to take a life—I had just never used it. We all have the ability to create life. That part is easy. But to take it, to destroy it, is something entirely different. And I had discovered that it wasn't difficult. At least not yet.

But time would tell. Would my mind dwell on it? Would my subconscious try to reason with me, to make me feel guilty? Or would it just become another memory, another moment in a growing collection?

"So, Robert was the first person you ever killed?" I asked.

"Yes," David answered. "He was the first. But over the next four years of traveling, there were many more."

I let his words settle, then exhaled. "Sounds like you became an addict."

"You could say that I was," David admitted. "I couldn't stop once I started. Killing gave me a high the rush of controlling someone's final moment. The power to decide when their life ends."

I raised an eyebrow. "What do you mean you were? You're still killing people, aren't you? Seems like you never stopped."

David's expression shifted, something unreadable flickering in his eyes. "I did stop," he said. "When I met Laura, I found a reason to stay in one place. A reason to stop traveling. And once I was with her, I didn't kill anyone else."

A smirk crossed my lips. "Laura does have a way of making life feel better."

"I thought so. It was good at first," David admitted. "But over time, the cracks started to show. The relationship wasn't perfect—not even close. Laura is difficult. She doesn't let you in

completely, and people come and go from her life like passing shadows. When she decides to move on, she just… moves. No hesitation. No second chances. Once she's gone, she's gone forever."

I exhaled, shaking my head. "So, what? Things fell apart, and just like someone who quits drinking but relapses when things get hard you went back to your old ways?"

David let out a sharp laugh. "Ha! You could call it 'David's End-Your-Life 2.0'—I'm joking," he said with a smirk. "It's not like that. Not anymore. Now, it's about more than just the rush."

His expression shifted, something darker settling behind his eyes.

"Before, killing in the shadows gave me a temporary high, but now… now it means something. It holds memory. Laura discarded Jake and Lucas left them like they never existed. To her, they were dead already. I just… finished the job." His voice was smooth, almost reflective, as if he were recounting a philosophical revelation rather than cold-blooded murder.

I felt something cold tighten in my stomach. "And the Asian man?" I asked cautiously.

David shrugged. "Collateral damage. He got caught in the crossfire of 'me.' Just another part of the grand myth of mankind we reach for so much, but we can never hold onto everything. That's the tragedy of existence."

His words should have unsettled me more than they did. But it was the next part that truly made my skin crawl.

"Just like I paid Borai for helping me with my first kill, I made donations in honor of the three men whose lives I took." His lips curled into a smirk. "For Jake, I donated to suicide prevention. For Nick, a generous sum went to gambling addiction recovery. And for Lucas" he let out a small chuckle, " the Houston Museum of Fine Arts received a healthy donation for his… artful death."

I narrowed my eyes. "Where are you going with all of this, David? What's your purpose? What's your exit plan?"

David leaned forward, his smirk widening. "Oh, I have a plan. I'll direct your friends here. And once all three blind mice are together again—" he paused for effect, his laughter low and deliberate, " I'll cut off their tails, just like the song goes."

I tensed.

David's gaze was cold, unwavering. "And since you don't have tails," he added, his grin sharpening, "your heads will have to suffice."

The end is sometimes nice

Laura and Peter sat in silence, still stunned, perched atop the observation deck at the Mount in McGovern Centennial Gardens. The day had shifted the damp, dewy morning air had given way to a crisp, dry coolness. The breeze brushed against their exposed arms, a contrast between warmth and chill. In the shade, the air carried just enough of a bite to warrant a light sweater or a thin jacket, but under the vast cobalt blue sky, where the sun streamed down in full force, its invisible heat blanketed their skin, dissolving the cold almost instantly.

Peter exhaled, pushing the code '3142' into David's burner phone. His fingers hovered over the screen as he scanned for anything any clue, any trace that might lead to Adam. It was a long shot, and he knew it, but it was all they had.

The frustration was suffocating. There are moments in life when no clear path presents itself, when every option feels useless, and the only thing worse than making the wrong decision is doing nothing at all. In times like these, the word waste seeps into our thoughts— "I can't believe I wasted this day already," or the quiet panic that comes when time slips through our fingers unnoticed: "This day passed by so fast… and what did I even do?" We measure our lives in moments, in minutes ticking by, in the illusion that time itself can be controlled. Yet, it's always slipping past us, shaping our routines around an invisible clock both real and imagined.

Peter broke the silence first. "There's nothing on this phone," he said, scrolling through the neatly organized screen. "But I will say David grouped his apps in a very structured way. He put them inside folders named by category, based on what the apps do."

Laura let out a small laugh, shaking her head. "Yeah, that's David. Obsessively organized. He hated clutter, hated chaos. Let me guess he has folders labeled 'News,' 'Social,' 'Travel' and so on?"

Peter glanced up at her, surprised. "Yeah!" He frowned slightly, turning the phone over in his hands. "But why would he be this organized with a burner phone? And more importantly— why would he direct us to it?"

"He likes games, and he's obviously confident he can beat us," Laura said, her voice steady but laced with frustration. "He's targeting me and anyone connected to me."

"Serial killers usually have a preferred type," Peter said, frowning as he processed the situation. "But this… this feels different. More like revenge than some compulsive need to relive a high. He's not just after a specific kind of victim he's after you."

"Maybe it's both," Laura murmured. "Maybe David is evolving."

She exhaled sharply, running a hand through her hair. "I told you before I always sensed something off about him, especially when he talked about his travels. I bet back then, he was like a typical serial killer learning, experimenting, perfecting his ability to kill and get away with it. The thrill. The rush. The satisfaction." She swallowed hard. "But after I ended things with him… it changed. Now it's personal. He's using his skills to get revenge, and he's targeting the people connected to me. I'm so sorry for bringing you and Adam into this nightmare."

"Don't say that," Peter said firmly. He reached over, wrapping an arm around her in a warm, steadying embrace. "This isn't your fault."

Laura looked at him, eyes softening. "Thank you," she whispered.

Her gaze lingered on his. Moist with emotion, her eyes seemed to pull Peter in like a quiet current. She moved closer whether it was instinct or gravity, she didn't know. And then, as if following an unspoken rhythm ingrained in human nature for thousands—perhaps millions—of years, their lips met.

Elsewhere…

Sitting in the same position for so long, I almost forgot I had legs.

There was no feeling from the waist down, no reminder of the dangling appendages except for the occasional tingling in my toes. It was strange how our bodies worked our fingers and toes twitched in small, erratic movements, even as the rest of us remained still, trapped in place by the weight of our own vessels.

I forced myself to focus. I needed to figure out where I was.

David had locked me up somewhere. A building, empty and lifeless. The stale air, the faint echo of silence, the gritty feel of dust beneath my fingers it felt like an abandoned office space. Maybe somewhere downtown, buried among other forgotten concrete husks, buildings left to decay in the shadows of a city that had outgrown them.

David wasn't here now. He hadn't been for hours at least; that's how it felt. But without a clock, a phone, or even the shifting of sunlight to guide me, time had lost all meaning.

It reminded me of a dream the kind where minutes stretch into hours, days even, only for you to wake up and realize mere moments had passed. The mind doesn't register time properly unless it has markers. Reading a book, watching a show, sitting through a meeting these things break the day into pieces, into something measurable.

But here? This was a meeting with no agenda, no scheduled end, no blocked-off calendar event to tell me when I'd be free.

All I had was the dim light filtering through whatever cracks existed in this building, just enough to make a guess. A feeling like those early mornings, waking up before my alarm, lying in bed, watching the darkness shift, trying to guess how much time I had left before the sound of my phone pulled me back into reality.

Only this time, there was no alarm waiting for me.

Alone in this stagnant space, where the air smelled faintly of mildew and old dust, I found my mind wandering through a series of random memories—though memories and thoughts often felt like the same thing. In a way, they were like stories we told ourselves, with us as both the audience and protagonist. We wove plots around our daily experiences, trying to place context and meaning on the world we perceived, making our small, immediate surroundings feel larger and more significant than they actually were.

My thoughts drifted to the nightmares I used to have as a child, often sparked by a scary movie that my older brother and father insisted on watching, even though I was clearly terrified. Maybe they thought it would make me braver, or maybe it was just their gentle version of torture, knowing my young mind would replay the violence at night. Whenever I lay in bed, darkness pressed in, and I was convinced the worst horrors were about to descend on me. It never made sense, but somehow certain parts of our home seemed to harbor these monsters—places where your imagination could fill every shadow with a creature waiting to strike.

The basement was the worst of all. The moment I stepped inside, my skin prickled, and every corner stretched into menacing shapes I couldn't quite see. The stairs, whether leading down to that basement or up to the higher floors, felt like runways I had to sprint along before some imaginary beast caught up. Even my own bedroom supposedly my haven became a labyrinth of creaking floorboards and faint, unexplainable noises once the lights went out. In the end, the only defense I could muster was to cower under a blanket, pretending I was asleep and hoping the monsters would feel pity and move on.

Eventually, I found a trick that seemed both obvious and surprisingly effective: focusing on happy movies, specifically Disney. I loved the feel-good energy of those cartoons Mickey Mouse, Donald Duck, Goofy, all of them. Each night, if I felt my anxieties rising, I'd mentally replay my favorite scenes. Like a personal bedtime story, it eased me away from terror and replaced it with a gentler world of laughter and bright colors. As I grew older, I didn't rely on Disney characters in quite the same way, but I kept the idea of escaping into a safe mental space a kind of meditation to help calm my mind whenever fear crept in.

Suddenly, the door creaked open, and David stepped in, his tone laced with mocking cheer. "Hello, dear I'm home. Did you miss me?"

I ignored his question and got straight to the point. "I could use a walk and a piss," I said flatly. "Some food and drink wouldn't hurt, either."

David chuckled. "Ah, no foreplay. Right to the punch. Lucky for you, I'm in a good mood, and I actually anticipated your… needs. So yes: walk, piss, food, and drink. All coming up."

"Where were you?" I asked, my voice more curious than aggressive. "Is Peter and Laura coming? I assume you know where they are."

"What's that saying— 'I could tell you, but then I'd have to kill you?'" David asked with an exaggerated laugh. "Well, I'm going to tell you and kill you. And your friends, too. They're still lost in Hermann Park, acting like lovebirds."

"What do you mean, lovebirds?" I asked, though I already had an uneasy hunch.

I tried to shake off the thought that Laura and Peter might actually be getting involved. But in moments of crisis, people sometimes cling to each other it's the "oh, shit" factor. And if Laura had to choose between me and Peter, it would probably be Peter. I knew that much.

David's grin sharpened. "Well, Laura seems to be sticking to her pattern of sleeping with every guy who wanders into her life," he said. "Jake, Lucas, yours truly, and now Peter. That makes four out of five. You could still be number five."

He paused, tapping his chin like a cartoon villain. "It makes sense. Lucas and Peter were both ambitious, confident types. You and Jake? The leftovers—the nice guys, the break from the drama."

I clenched my jaw. "And what does that make you?"

David spread his arms wide. "A good question. I'm unique: creative, artistic, passionate, brilliant, athletic… oh, the list goes on."

"You're certainly full of yourself," I said, glaring.

He shrugged, not at all bothered. "Her loss, leaving me. And it's cost her, more than she'll ever realize."

Meanwhile, at Hermann Park…

Lisa.

She was the first thought in Peter's mind the moment he kissed Laura. He hadn't been with another woman since losing Lisa and moving to Houston—hadn't even considered it. The pain was still fresh, not at all scabbed over, even though it'd been more than a year.

Now, as Laura's lips met his, that pain rushed back, a bruised heart throbbing with every reminder of Lisa. Yet at the same time, something else stirred in him a warmth, a tentative hope.

Time can heal, but it's a slow medicine that doesn't always work. Sometimes it takes another person to truly stitch up the wounds. And in that kiss, in the soft press of Laura's mouth against his, Peter felt his heart open, allowing her inside. Laura's kiss became the drug he needed to pull him from the shadows he'd been living in since Lisa's death.

"What?" Peter muttered, feeling his phone vibrate.

"It's your phone," Laura pointed out. "Is it David again?"

Peter glanced at the screen. "No, it's a text from my boss," he said, grimacing. "He wants me at the precinct right away."

Laura nodded, concern edging into her eyes. "Then go. I don't want you getting into trouble."

Peter shook his head. "I don't want to leave you behind. Come with me. I can't risk what happened before—" he paused, his voice quivering. "I can't lose someone else. It's too painful."

Laura squeezed his hand. "I'm not going to die like Lisa. I promise. I'll stay here in the park, where there are crowds. David won't try anything with so many people around. I'll be careful."

Peter exhaled, his relief tinged with reluctance. "Alright. I'll be quick—no detours." He pulled her into a brief kiss before hurrying away, casting one last anxious glance over his shoulder.

Meanwhile…

My hate hasn't dulled; it's only grown sharper. I thought I'd be numb by now, that I'd have pushed it all aside. But hate seems like my best solution my guard against everything that's wrong in my life. Some people chase love. That's too complicated. I tried it with Laura, thinking I could change my path. But my parents raised me to find my own goals, and I discovered my true calling in that alley in Cambodia, with Robert.

He showed me how anger and hate can forge me into my best possible self—feeding my ambition the way flesh sustains our bodies. Life is violent. We slaughter animals to eat, to live. My killing of people is no different. It's how I survive. I'll finally feel whole once I finish what I started in New Orleans, ending it here in Houston with three more kills—fueled by all my lingering hate.

"Waiting is hard, isn't it?" David asked, snapping me out of my thoughts. He sounded almost casual, like he was talking about a delayed flight. "I get so impatient, but I remind myself to let the plan unfold in its own time."

I frowned. "What exactly are we waiting for?"

"Your friends, of course!" David said with exaggerated cheer. "That's what I meant about waiting. Peter is clever smarter than you or Laura, anyway. He might figure out my clues. Or maybe he won't. That's what makes life fun sometimes the unknown, the suspense, the what ifs. It keeps the heart racing and the nerves on high alert."

I stared at him. "Don't you ever worry about getting caught? Or about what your parents would think? You clearly don't care that it's wrong immoral."

David smirked. "I've killed over a hundred people. I don't get caught. I always see my exit before I act. Every last detail is meticulously planned." He shrugged. "As for my parents, why would I care? It's my life, not theirs. I don't need their approval or anyone else's. I only look inward, draw my strength from the deepest part of me. I'm a true introvert that way."

I shook my head. "Everyone slips up at least once. You're not infallible."

He laughed, the sound as sharp as broken glass. "That's the fun, isn't it? The chance that maybe someone will find a crack in my armor. Let's call that hope. The lingering feeling that you or your friends still have a shot at something good happening. A miracle, if you want to be dramatic." His grin widened. "They're probably hoping that second phone of mine will lead them straight to me. Let them try. It'll be entertaining to see how it all plays out."

"So, does it?" I asked, my voice tight. "Or is it just another trick you're adding to the board to wear everyone out?"

David shrugged, gazing off with a distant, almost bored expression. "Honestly, that phone is old. I can't remember everything I left on it. Between New Orleans and coming here to Houston, I was juggling both phones, trying to stitch together all these plans. Maybe I left something on it… maybe not. It's too late now, anyway." He let out a slow breath, his tone turning ominous. "This is the fun part—seeing if your friends can follow my breadcrumbs. If they don't, I'll have to spoon-feed them, lead them right to you so I can kill the lot of you together. The real question is: who do I kill first?" He paused, a grin creeping across his face. "Obvious, isn't it? You'll be the last. I want you to watch your friends die, my final three masterpieces. Then maybe I'll retire after my grand finale."

Meanwhile, at the Precinct…

Peter's phone buzzed again, and he saw Bruce's name pop up like a summons. Being a detective meant you were never truly off the clock—twenty-four hours a day, three-sixty-five a year. It wasn't a surprise, but he couldn't help the uneasy twist in his gut.

He had a job to do, leads to chase, and precious little time—especially with David still out there. But no matter how autonomous he felt, he still had to answer to Bruce, the lieutenant who held the reins.

"What did we agree on about checking in with me at the end of every day?" Bruce demanded the moment Peter stepped into his office. His voice was sharp, like the snap of a whip. "I've given you a long leash, son. Don't make me yank it short—and fit it with a choke collar, too."

Peter swallowed. Bruce was in a sour mood, likely from all the press coverage on the serial killer case. The higher-ups had probably landed on Bruce's back, applying pressure from way above. That pressure rolled downhill, and Peter felt it settle squarely on his shoulders, the final stop on its way down the chain of command.

He clenched his jaw, remembering what a friend had once told him—a boss who loved quoting The Outlaw Josey Wales, always muttering, "Don't piss down my back and tell me it's raining."

He forced a steady nod. "Understood, sir. I'll keep you informed daily."

Yet as he left the office, the back of his neck was damp with sweat. David was still out there, somewhere, weaving his twisted game. And Peter had to find him fast before any more lives were destroyed.

"Sorry, Bruce, for not reporting in," I said, trying not to sound too defensive.

"It's been three days," Bruce reminded me, his tone stern but not hostile. "You know the rules just a daily check-in. I could be a real hardass and demand end-of-day reports, but all I'm asking for is a simple email, call, or text."

"I know, and I'm sorry." I sighed. "I just didn't have anything to say. From now on, even if it's 'nothing to report,' I'll let you know."

"Good!" Bruce said, leaning back in his chair. "I called you in because I have a new assignment. There's this guy in Houston who explores abandoned places—old office buildings, malls, factories wherever. I want you to follow up."

I frowned. "Bruce, I've got other things on my plate. Can't you give it to someone else?"

Bruce gave me that look like a parent shooting down your protest before you even finish talking. The silent "I'm your boss; this isn't up for debate."

"He's on Instagram under the name 'Nighthawkhouston'," Bruce continued.

"You mean his handle?" I corrected gently. "It's '@Nighthawkhouston.'"

"Whatever," Bruce grunted. "Just find him. Talk to him. If he's poking around empty buildings, maybe he's seen something that can help us with the mess piling up on my desk."

I forced a nod. "Got it."

But I had my own priorities. First, I had to check on Laura and make sure she was safe. Luckily, there weren't any cameras in Bruce's office to record me bolting out on personal business. If he knew how much time I was splitting between work and my private life, he'd tear me a new one.

Once I knew Laura was alright, I could do a little digging on this Nighthawkhouston guy. That was the beauty of modern police work—so many leads could be checked online before ever knocking on someone's door.

Memory Lane

It's funny how time feels linear, yet we loop back to old memories without warning. Suddenly, I was back in the hot, humid summers of North Carolina, biking around with my best friend, Mike Thompson. We'd spend entire days roaming the neighborhood, seeing what everyone else was up to shooting hoops or tearing through the trails in the woods behind the houses on Barwick Drive.

Every day, we ended up at the local convenience store aptly named "Local Mart." That's where I discovered the simple joy of cherry Coke and Hostess Crunch Donettes. Even after all these years, remembering that first taste brought a tiny smile to my face, reminding me how some things were so easy back then and how quickly they fade into the past.

I loved the rush of discovering something on my own like the day I spotted that cherry Coke and a pack of coconut mini donuts in the local convenience store. Nobody told me to buy them; it was pure chance. My eyes roamed the rows of neon-colored snacks, each shining in harsh fluorescent light on metal shelves. Everything looked tempting, but most choices seemed too bright, too sugary, too gimmicky. Then I saw the donuts—plain white, dusted with coconut flakes. Simple and perfect.

Refrigeration at its finest existed in that store, with vacuum-sealed glass doors filled with crisp, ice-cold soda. I remember the satisfying whoosh of cold air that escaped when I opened one, the kind that makes your skin tingle. Reaching in and grabbing that dark, carbonated elixir felt like a personal triumph. It was a gamble—picking something new always was. But I never regretted that choice. The memory lodged into my mind, weaving itself into the fabric of all those other decisions and small victories that would form my life's tapestry.

"Adam, daydreaming again?" David's voice cut through my thoughts. He stood there, arms folded, wearing a crooked grin.

"Nothing important," I said, shaking off the past. "Just childhood memories."

"How sweet." His smile turned mocking. "A first kiss, maybe? A fun family vacation? Do tell."

I gave him a flat stare. "It was nothing. I'm done with my little trip down memory lane."

David chuckled. "So sensitive today. But you should be happy. I've kept you alive longer than anyone else. You're my new record quite an accomplishment. Must be your connection to Laura, right?"

I rolled my eyes. "Guess I should say thanks… for my future dying."

"See?" David laughed. "Now we're having fun. But you're becoming a bore. Time to liven things up. Maybe a woman's touch will help. Laura will be the perfect guest."

My heart lurched. "What the hell are you talking about?" I demanded. "You think you can just snatch her? Peter's with her he won't let that happen. You can't do anything you want, no matter how unstoppable you think you are."

David's smile was cold. "Oh, but I can."

"Oh, Adam you really underestimate me," David said, shaking his head with a theatrical sigh. "I guess that's the world we live in. Even if people see your past work, they treat it like its ancient history. No one ever thinks you can still create something new. Your track record counts for nothing. I have to prove myself over and over again."

I bristled, my voice snapping with urgency. "Where are you going?"

David's eyes glinted with amusement. "I'm going to get our friend, Laura—just like I told you I would."

The blood pounded in my ears. Gone were the warm, nostalgic memories I'd been nursing. Now my mind churned with fear for Laura and Peter. David had left, presumably to set his twisted plan in motion. I couldn't stay here, tied up and helpless. I needed a plan, even a small one step that might lead to another. If I gave in to hopelessness, I'd never find a way out. But I was blank, and every option felt sealed behind locked doors.

Sometimes, when cornered like this, I come up with little phrases cheesy mantras to get me through. Or I think them up and then hope they make sense later. The only words that came to mind were, "The end is sometimes nice."

Laura, meanwhile, sat cross-legged in the park's-tired grass, the late-afternoon sun casting lazy shadows around her. She absently slid her fingertips along the blades, noticing how the dark green faded to yellow at the tips a reminder of how everything, no matter how vibrant, could wither with time.

Faces drifted through her thoughts: the men who had shaped her life, both here and gone. Above all of them stood her father. She remembered every dinner they shared, even the quiet ones when they barely spoke. He had this gift for lifting the day's heaviness—like injecting helium into a conversation so that any gloom just floated away. People gravitated to him, wanting to bask in that buoyancy, if only for a little while.

She could still picture the last trip they took together, about a month before he died— offshore deep-sea fishing on the coast. He always found ways to make each week special for her, encouraging new experiences and adventures. If Laura voiced an interest in something, he'd leap at the chance to make it happen. And if she drew a blank, he'd surprise her with spontaneous plans—impromptu outings that turned into cherished memories they'd recount at the dinner table. Each excursion became a story they carried home, one more precious moment to reminisce about in the days and years ahead.

Even the times you thought you didn't want to remember could still bring an instant smile whenever the story was retold. That final fishing trip with her father was exactly like that for Laura—an experience that should have been a disaster, yet somehow turned into one of her favorite memories. She and her father had packed an absurd amount of snacks and drinks, anticipating a long day of hooking big fish and savoring every moment together. There would be hours of companionable silence, rods in hand, with plenty of breaks for good conversation whenever they felt like talking. But even when they just sat together, watching the horizon for any sign of a catch, Laura felt perfectly at peace—her father's presence radiated comfort and calm.

In hindsight, everything about that day screamed storm warning. The wind whipped across the water, churning what should have been gentle swells into sudden, choppy waves capped with white foam. The boat rocked so wildly it seemed like a pendulum stuck on a horizontal swing. Despite all the food they had so eagerly brought, neither Laura nor her father could stomach a single bite; it took every ounce of willpower not to lose the little breakfast they'd had earlier. And as if the sea hadn't taken enough from them, not a single fish touched their lines. They returned to shore empty-handed and queasy, but the second they were back in the car, they were already laughing spinning the ordeal into larger-than-life tales of seasickness and heroic (if imaginary) feats. By the time they got home, that "terrible day" had become one more cherished story in their shared collection.

Yet so many men in Laura's life had left too soon. She thought of her father, of Jake, of Lucas. To be fair, she had left Jake and Lucas on her own terms, choosing different paths when their relationships had run their course. She could have tried to reconnect later, but time and distance had widened the gap. It was like looking at an old photo: a frozen moment, forever stuck in the past. And now, it was too late; they were gone, just like her father.

Still, Laura reminded herself, there were three men in her life now. Peter, her friend who was quickly becoming something more, someone she could imagine growing old with. Adam, the friend who had so much to offer the world, the one she desperately hoped to save before tragedy struck again. And then there was David, that stranger from her past who once meant more to her than she cared to admit—a man she had tried to leave behind, only to find he wouldn't let her go.

There she is relaxing in the grass as though she hasn't a care in the world. Sometimes, when you stop fearing danger, it's the very moment it comes rushing in. It blindsides you, sets your heart racing, makes your insides quiver like there's an electric current running under your skin. Plenty of trees here in the park for me to stay out of sight. I can angle my approach toward Laura without her suspecting what's about to happen. Game. Sport. Life. It's all angles. If you can't see the angles the ones you've taken and the ones you will take, you'll never succeed. People who don't think about their paths, both present and past, just drift through life like hollow shells, mere chemical reactions bouncing from one step to the next.

"Did you miss me?" David's voice sliced through the quiet. It came from behind a nearby tree.

Laura tensed. "David?" she echoed, her tone riddled with uncertainty.

She spun around, searching for him. Her mind was still churning through thoughts of David how often in life do we think of someone, only for them to suddenly appear or text or call? It's like the world is coded to respond to our private thoughts, a cosmic algorithm that recognizes our mental searches. Maybe it's mere chance, or maybe we're all under constant surveillance, our every notion funneled through some invisible script.

"A shame Peter left you here all alone," David said, stepping out from the shadows.

"He had to go to work," Laura said, chin lifting in defiance. "I told him to leave."

David's lip curled. "You thought staying here in the park would be safe?" He let out a low laugh. "Haven't you and your friends figured out I can do anything? Public spaces don't protect you. I've been doing this for years, all over the world. Now, I like to think of myself as a… public artist."

"So what?" Laura pressed, feeling her pulse spike. "You're going to kill me right here?"

"Oh no," David said, shaking his head casually. "Not here. Not yet. We're going back to your friend, Adam. Call it a happy reunion with the men in your life."

Laura blinked, relief and dread warring in her eyes. "Adam's… still alive?"

"Yes, Adam is safe he's not my type," David said with a smirk. "Besides, I'm not quite inspired yet. I need… proper motivation to finish all the work I have to do. Speaking of which, we should get moving before your new love shows up and spoils our reunion."

Laura's heart hammered. "What if I scream?" she asked, voice tight. "I can fight you until Peter comes back. Then we'll see if you can handle us both."

David's expression remained disturbingly calm. "Then I'd kill you right here, right now," he said, his tone flat. "It'd be a shame, really dying in such a boring way, not even part of my grand display around this city. At least if you cooperate, you'll have the chance to see Adam. Maybe you can save him. I'm giving you the sliver of hope humans always cling to. Very American of me, don't you think? Animals kill all the time and we humans do it more than any other species."

"Okay, enough with your bullshit," Laura spat, her resolve settling in. "I'll go."

David was right about hope. A strange sense of resolve welled inside Laura. She and Peter had been spinning in circles for too long, finding no trace of Adam or David. Now, suddenly, David appeared this horrifying stranger from her past. Yet, for the first time, she saw a path forward: a chance to save Adam and end David's menace forever. Of all the men she'd left behind in her life, this bastard was the only one she wanted to truly see gone dead, not just vanished.

As if reading her thoughts, David's gaze flickered with amusement. "Laura, you forgot something," he said. "One last thing."

She tensed. "What's that?"

His grin widened. "Throw your phone on the ground. Let's leave Peter a little gift something for him to find, something dramatic. We wouldn't want him missing out on our fun."

Peter kept repeating one thought in his head: I'm coming. But the traffic around him moved at a crawl like cars slogging through molasses instead of gliding effortlessly on air. He was still minutes from Hermann Park, and Laura wasn't answering any of his calls or texts. Pressure weighed on him from all sides: work demands piling up and, more critically, a deranged killer gunning for Laura and possibly for him as well.

It's not just Laura he wants, Peter reminded himself. He wants me too. And Adam, if he hasn't killed him already. The nerve-jangling silence from Laura only fueled his panic. Why wasn't she picking up her phone?

With a quick glance, he grabbed his own phone, pulling up a location-tracking app. Under normal circumstances, he'd never violate her privacy, but this was a life-or-death emergency. He located her signal: just outside the McGovern Centennial Gardens, deeper into Hermann Park's tangle of paths, grass, and trees. It struck him—This isn't the dusty desert my friends in California picture when they think of Texas. Houston was lush, almost swampy in places, with thick grass and towering trees. But she's here somewhere, he thought, and I have to find her.

When he arrived at the spot, panic gripped him: no sign of Laura. He called her name, voice echoing in the open expanse. "Laura!" he shouted, hoping for her to pop out from behind a tree, to wave him over. Please let her be safe. But there was no answer—only the rustling of leaves in the breeze.

Then he spotted it: a phone in the grass. Sprinting over, he snatched it up. His heart sank like a stone when he realized it was Laura's phone.

The weight of it felt crushing in his hand, every second packing on dread. His mind suddenly flashed back to California, the day he raced to Venice Beach—only to find Lisa's car wrecked, to learn she was gone. Not again, he thought. Not another woman I care about, dying before I can save her. He was supposed to protect them—he was the detective. He was the one trained to handle danger.

But in this moment, he felt utterly helpless. And hopeless. Laura and Adam were in mortal peril, and he had no direct way to save them. He'd lost Lisa, and he might lose two more people he cared about. The heartbreak felt like it would split him apart. I barely survived Lisa's death. How can I survive losing two at once?

Last time, I drove like a madman, blindly chasing that van. I was convinced it held the people who took everything I loved. Now, I couldn't even bring myself to stand and chase the ghost David who was ripping apart the pieces of my life. Instead, I just collapsed onto the grass in Hermann Park a place that's supposed to offer relief from the city's concrete sprawl, where people come to breathe fresh air and enjoy the wind rustling through the trees.

But I felt no relief. My mind spun in a hundred directions at once, lighting up with desperate ideas I couldn't fully grasp. It was like being lost in those childhood magazine mazes—the flimsy, off-white pages with black-lined paths you'd trace with a worn pencil, looking for an unblocked route but hitting dead ends over and over. Every potential solution felt like a dead end, leading nowhere but frustration.

Where do ideas come from anyway? Some chemical chain reaction sparks in the brain, lodging itself in the shelves of our neurons, until we hear ourselves say, "That's a good idea—let's try it." Suddenly, clarity flickered through the dark swirl of my thoughts. My gaze fell on the three phones I held in my hands. I also had my detective walkie and more walkies in the car. My boss, Bruce, would be expecting some kind of update soon, probably by phone, text, or both.

I hadn't opened Instagram in a while. I usually avoided the barrage of travel shots, food pics, and tablescapes paired with fine wine contemporary versions of 17th-century still-life paintings, all moody fruits and wine goblets. A modern twist, yes, but sometimes just as lifeless.

Still, I remembered Bruce's lead. I sighed, opened the app, and typed in the search bar: "Nighthawkhouston." The profile popped up, complete with post count, followers, and following lists none of which I cared about. My only focus was on the photos and descriptions he'd shared, any clue that might guide me toward David, Laura, and Adam. There, on my phone screen, was Nighthawkhouston and maybe the key to this whole nightmare.

The posts showed abandoned malls, small office buildings, hospitals, and even movie theaters. All of them, once bustling, were now dark and empty failed ventures or relocations had turned these modern ruins into a kind of urban wilderness. People like "Nighthawkhouston" crawled through them like explorers in a new-age cave system, documenting every broken window and echoing corridor. A part of me wondered why the homeless didn't turn these vacant spaces into little cities of their own—a haven for those left behind by the capitalist churn. But in the pictures I was seeing, none of these places looked like the site of David's recent attacks. They were all on Houston's outskirts, while David's chaos—kidnapping Laura and stalking the rest of us— had centered around the city's core.

One post, however, caught my attention. It was older, dated about two months ago, and featured a forty-five-story skyscraper on Bell Street in downtown Houston—what used to be the Exxon Tower. Exxon had abandoned it for a sleek new campus up north in The Woodlands, leaving the old building vacant. I remembered telling Laura about that exact area when we first discussed the string of incidents happening in Houston's central districts.

Thinking about David's phone, I wondered if he'd left any trace that tied him to "Nighthawkhouston" and possibly the Exxon Tower. He had such a methodical way of organizing his apps it might be my best shot at finding a clue. I flipped through the neatly labeled folders on his screen until I reached one simply named "Social." If David had anything connecting him to the urban explorer, it would be in there.

Opening the folder, I saw the usual suspects: Facebook, X, WhatsApp, and then the bold, multi-hued icon of Instagram. I tapped it, relieved to see David had stayed logged in. His feed was mostly typical social media fare: travel snapshots, scenic vistas, and reminders of all the places he'd been. It all seemed so mundane for someone capable of such terrifying acts.

Then, tucked between shots of beaches and city skylines, I found the link I was looking for a post of an empty movie theater taken by "Nighthawkhouston." David had liked it. Scrolling further, I found a post featuring the Exxon Tower and, sure enough, David had liked that one as well. There it was: the direct connection between David's Instagram and "Nighthawkhouston," right where I hoped it would be.

Then my skin prickled the moment I noticed the message bubble in the top-right corner of my Instagram screen. The sideways lightning bolt, glowing a dull red, signaled that there were unread messages waiting for me messages that I was both anxious and afraid to see. With a quick tap, I found myself staring at a long series of exchanges between David and someone calling himself "Nighthawkhouston."

As I read, my worst suspicions solidified: David had asked this urban explorer pointed questions about the Exxon Tower how to get inside without being noticed, what kind of security (if any) was stationed there, and whether an intruder could simply walk in and stay indefinitely. From the conversation, it was frighteningly clear that the building was basically wide open. There were no guards, no barriers, and barely even a locked door to dissuade trespassers.

In that moment, I felt my heartbeat stutter. If David was actively seeking such details, there was a strong chance he was already inside that very skyscraper. With Laura and Adam both missing, it made grim sense that the Exxon Tower might now be his hideout—a place where he could operate unseen, free to do whatever he pleased. Before dashing off to confront him, though, I realized I needed more information from the source: this "Nighthawkhouston" character.

I switched over to my personal Instagram account, found and followed his profile, and immediately sent him a direct message. I could tell from his prior chats with David—and from the sheer amount of time he seemed to spend conversing with his followers—that this Nighthawk was a sociable guy, likely to respond fast. Sure enough, within minutes a new notification popped up.

Nighthawkhouston: What's up, Peter? Thanks for following me on Insta!

He sounded casual, almost friendly, which only made me more aware of how high the stakes were.

Me: No problem. Nice to meet you. What's your name?

Nighthawkhouston: You can just call me Nighthawk. Any posts of mine you wanna chat about?

I exhaled. There was no time to dance around the issue.

Me: Look, I need your real name. This is urgent it's about the Exxon Tower.

He seemed taken aback by my directness.

Nighthawkhouston: Bruh, I don't give my name to just anyone!

Me: I'm a detective here in Houston. If you don't cooperate, I'll bring you into the precinct and interrogate the living hell out of you.

A pause followed a few heartbeats of tense silence then a frantic reply:

Nighthawkhouston: Oh, fuck! My name's Bobby Singleton. What do you want from me?

Me: Call me right now at this number: 832-546-6886.

As I hit "send," my pulse pounded. I couldn't help picturing Laura and Adam in that towering, vacant building dark corridors, empty offices, and endless places for David to hide them away from the outside world. If Bobby Singleton could offer any insight, I had to squeeze it out of him. David was methodical, cunning, and chillingly confident. Every second I spent hunting for answers was another second he could use to set his deadly plan in motion.

I prayed Bobby would call soon and tell me something that could break this wide open. If the Exxon Tower was truly as unguarded as the messages suggested, David would have no trouble keeping his captives there. My only hope was that this lead might let me beat him to the punch, stopping another murder before it was too late.

My phone rang almost immediately—Bobby didn't waste a second before calling. He was just as quick with a phone call as he'd been with his Instagram messages, which was a good sign.

I already knew I'd need his help to pull off the plan rapidly forming in my mind as I made my way toward the Exxon Tower.

"Hi, Bobby," I answered, forcing a calm tone despite the chaos swirling inside me.

"What do you want, man?" he said in a voice that conveyed both curiosity and exasperation.

"My boss asked me to track you down," I began, "and look into your hobby of sneaking into abandoned places around Houston. But I'm not here to arrest you. I don't have the time or the desire to bust you for trespassing. The truth is, we've been after a serial killer in Houston—someone you might know as the 'code-blooded killer.' He's one of your followers on Instagram, and I think he used your posts about the Exxon Tower as inspiration. I'm almost certain he's there right now, holding two of my friends hostage."

"Bruh, seriously?" Bobby exclaimed. "You mean that psycho who's been on the news? The 'code-blooded killer?'"

"Yeah, that's him," I confirmed. "His name is David. He's following you under the handle 'Davidpresentworldseen,' and he's asked you about the Exxon Tower in your DMs. Check your messages."

I heard a few clicks as Bobby presumably fiddled with his phone. Then a sudden gasp. "Holy shit. It's him. The actual killer. On my message thread. Jesus Christ."

"Listen carefully, Bobby," I said firmly, hoping my seriousness got through. "I need to get to the Exxon Tower as soon as possible, but before I do, I need you to do a couple of things. First, come to Hermann Park. I'm going to bury one of my police walkies under the fourth bush to the left of the McGovern Centennial Gardens entrance. Grab it. Once you have it, text me so I know you're good. Then drive straight to 1900 Rusk Street—that's the Houston Police Precinct. Go to the detective division, ask for Bruce Scott, my boss, and tell him that Peter sent you. Hand over the walkie and tell him I'm going after the 'code-blooded killer.' Got it?"

"Yeah, okay," Bobby said, sounding equal parts spooked and eager to help. "I'll message you once I get it."

"Perfect. Talk soon," I told him, ending the call.

As I hung up, my mind began looping the same thoughts in a maddening cycle. My brain felt a hundred steps ahead already envisioning the Exxon Tower, scanning its floors, anticipating what David might do next while my body sat behind the wheel, driving in relative silence through Houston's crowded streets. The mental dissonance was unnerving, as though my mind raced on without my permission while the rest of me was stuck in the present.

I forced a deep breath, reminding myself not to let my anxiety run the show. Step by step. I had a plan one I needed to see through. As long as I stayed focused, I stood a chance of catching David at his own game. I needed to channel the calm fortitude I'd inherited from my great-great-great-grandfather, Paul, who'd once tracked down an escaped prison gang after the Convict Lake murders. This was my moment, and I intended to save Laura and Adam, no matter what it took.

From our vantage point on the forty-fifth floor of this sixty-year-old concrete monolith, I couldn't help wondering how many decades of sunrises and sunsets had passed over the people once working here thousands of souls worrying about their little lives while the world kept rolling on with a kind of indifferent stoicism. Now, in this abandoned skyscraper, it was Laura's turn to see Adam again.

"Adam!" Laura cried, obvious relief flooding her voice the moment she spotted me. "You're alive... Are you okay? Did he hurt you?"

"I'm fine," I replied, managing a small smile to reassure her.

"Laura, have a seat next to Adam," David ordered, his tone cold. "You two can catch up once you're tied down like he is, nice and firm in your chair."

I glanced at Laura, guilt and anger mingling inside me. "How did he even find you?"

She exhaled. "Peter and I were at Hermann Park, looking for your other phone. We found it, but then he got a call from work. David showed up while Peter was gone and... convinced me to come here."

David let out a mocking laugh. "Ha! You found the phone. Adorable. I guided every step you and Peter made. I knew exactly when he'd leave you to speak with his boss. Just like I know right now he's on his way up here with all three phones. He's not much of a detective if he forgets that 'Find My' GPS is enabled on each device. I can see his every move. Credit where it's due, though he's cleverer than I expected, managing to figure out where I am. If he were really smart, he'd turn those phones off or disable GPS so he could sneak in here. But no. Instead, he's showing me exactly where he is, trying to save you two."

Privately, I hoped Bobby would find the walkie I left for him soon. It was one of a thousand worries spinning through my head right now. The next thought was about turning off the phones so I could go "invisible" to David's digital eyes. I knew I was heading straight for the Exxon Tower, and David was tracking me every mile of the way. If I suddenly disappeared from his map, he might decide to flee with Laura and Adam—or worse, kill them on the spot before I could arrive.

No, better to keep the phones on. Let him think he's in control, that he's still the one orchestrating everything. I briefly considered leaving one or all of the phones back at Hermann Park to confuse him, but I realized I needed David to believe he knew my location at all times. Once I made it inside this desolate tower, I could separate each phone, placing them in different corners, forcing him to search me out in a twisted game of hide-and-seek. If he was so certain of his power, I wanted to use that confidence against him and hope I could turn the tables before he had the chance to hurt Laura or Adam again.

"Hello?" I answered, forcing my voice to sound calmer than I felt.

"It's me, Bobby," came the reply. "I found the walkie you left for me. Now you want me to take it to your boss. Does he even know I'm coming?"

"Good work, Bobby," I said, relieved he was following through. "No, I haven't told him you'd be dropping off the walkie. I can't call him right now—he'd try to take over the operation, and I have my own plan. So, you bring him that walkie. Turn it on, and switch it to channel four. Got it?"

"Yeah, yeah. I got it," he muttered. "Feels like some crappy errand you got me on."

"Hey, at least you're not risking your life the way I am," I shot back.

He paused, then his voice brightened with urgency. "Oh, wait I remembered something. Looking back at the messages I had with that killer… he kept asking about the forty-fifth-floor conference room at the Exxon Tower. He loved the photos I posted especially the windows. He was real curious about the layout. Thought you'd wanna know."

"That's helpful. Thanks, Bobby," I said. "I'll know when you've delivered the walkie my boss will be calling to tear me a new one for keeping him in the dark. Good luck."

I ended the call, my mind roiling with new worries. Laura was right next to me, tied up, but there might be a slim chance we could talk privately even if only for a moment. I had things to tell her. But David's looming presence made true conversation impossible. He had a habit of popping in, mocking us, and I needed him distracted long enough to share crucial info with Laura.

"You two lovebirds sit tight," David joked from across the room. "Oops—maybe I should say 'friends,' since apparently Laura's got another mouse she's smitten with. You two must have a lot to discuss, considering all that's happened."

I turned to Laura. "We need to distract him," I whispered.

"What?" Her eyes flicked between me and David. "Distract him how? And why?"

I glanced over at David. He was glued to his phone, probably monitoring Peter's location through the GPS. "He keeps tracking Peter on those phones. Peter's leaving them on for a reason—probably to trick David. We need to buy Peter more time. David's a talker; if we can get him to ramble, he'll stop obsessing over his phone."

Laura's expression hardened. "So, we rile him up, get him bragging?"

"Exactly. David's arrogant he believes he can't lose. We just need to hammer the idea he might lose. Tell him Peter's better, smarter, that David's not as invincible as he thinks."

"You sure that won't make him kill us on the spot?" she asked, voice hushed.

"He's planning to kill us anyway," I reminded her. "But this way, we at least stand a chance. Just follow my lead when he comes back."

Meanwhile, outside the Exxon Tower…

I parked a few blocks away, trying to come up with a plan to enter the building unnoticed. A giant rectangular skyscraper has limited 'backways,' but there had to be some service entrance for deliveries, or a garbage area I could slip through. If the conference room was on the forty-fifth floor overlooking Buffalo Bayou near the I-10 freeway, it would likely face north or west. That meant I should approach from the south to avoid being spotted from above—David could be scanning the streets through the windows or, worse, tracking me via GPS on the phones I carried.

Still, I couldn't kill the GPS signals yet. If David realized he'd lost me on his map, he might bolt or worse, take out Laura and Adam before I arrived. The best approach was to keep the phones on, let him think he was in control, then hide them somewhere inside once I got in. With any luck, I'd turn David's overconfidence into an advantage and find Laura and Adam before it was too late.

"Peter!" Bruce's voice crackled through my walkie, carrying its usual tone of frustration.

I had brought two walkies from my car along with the three phones, each device part of a plan I was piecing together in real time.

"What the hell are you doing?" Bruce continued, practically roaring into my ear. "I've got that punk 'Nighthawkhouston'—right here, the guy I told you to go talk to. He just handed me a walkie he claims you told him to deliver."

"Great. That means Bobby made it to you," I replied, feeling a small surge of relief.

"Jesus, bruh, why you gotta spill my name like that?" Bobby grumbled in the background, his exasperation audible. "Just leave me here bleeding in the street, giving out my name and blowing my cover."

"Shut the hell up!" Bruce barked, and I could picture him glaring in Bobby's direction, veins pulsing at his temple. Even though I wasn't there in person, I could feel the weight of Bruce's wrath being directed at the urban explorer.

"Peter, you better hurry your ass back here with some good explanation," Bruce growled. "Because right now, I've got half a mind to toss both you and Bobby behind bars until I get some answers."

"Bruce, just keep channel four open," I said firmly. "Bobby has valuable information on the code-blooded killer's hideout. He can fill you in on whatever you need to know. I'm in the middle of trying to capture the guy."

"Not your case, Peter!" Bruce roared. "You give me the killer's name—right now—and I'll come with backup. We'll do this by the book."

"I can't do that, sorry," I answered, my voice clipped.

"Goddammit, Peter!" Bruce bellowed, anger radiating off every syllable. "That's a direct order! You disobey, you're finished as a detective!"

"He'll kill my friends if you come anywhere near him with a squad," I said, my tone unyielding. "He's taken two people I care about—he knows us, personally. I can't risk him losing it if he sees cops on every corner. Just keep the walkie on. I'll check in when I can."

"Peter! Peter!" Bruce's shouts dissolved into a harsh static as I turned the volume down on both walkies, no longer needing his voice hammering at my ears.

I was nearly at the loading dock behind the Exxon Tower. The wide, low-hanging entry was shadowed by overhanging metal siding and flanked by dumpsters. The air smelled of stale grease and old cardboard. This was where trucks once delivered office supplies back when this place was buzzing with suited workers, not hosting a madman.

David's laughter cut across the silence of the forty-fifth-floor conference room, where Laura and Adam were bound to chairs.

"Okay, what were you two whispering about?" he asked, strolling into the room with a mocking grin. "I assume I was the topic of conversation—obviously."

"Actually," Adam said, lifting his head to address David, "I was telling Laura I think you've finally met your match."

David's brow furrowed, but he retained that self-assured smirk. "Peter? You can't possibly be serious. That boy can't and won't beat me. In fact, I'm looking forward to killing him in front of you both. Maybe then you'll see who's really better."

Adam tipped his chin in Laura's direction, inviting her to continue. She drew a breath, choosing her words carefully to bait David's ego. "Adam's right," she said, letting a hint of doubt slip into her voice. "Peter told me a story from his days in Los Angeles someone close to him was murdered, and he tracked down the killers, then slaughtered them like it was nothing. I guess you could say he's… experienced. Brutal, even."

"You're both acting like I'm some novice," David scoffed, irritation flaring in his eyes. "Laura, I never told you the details of what I did before we met, because if you knew half of it, you'd probably have run sooner. I've killed over a hundred men all across the globe. The media stamps me with 'Code-Blooded Killer,' but that barely scratches the surface. I'm an artist a traveler carving out my legacy. That first kill, your buddy Jake, was just a public introduction. I left that message on his chest, but the press twisted it into some 'computer-code murder' story. It's a joke. If I had to pick a better name, I'd want something like 'Traveler Killer' or 'Artistic Killer.' I am no tech nerd butchering people for lines of code."

He paused, crossing his arms, clearly enjoying the sound of his own voice. Laura and Adam exchanged a quick glance, both hoping their little provocation was succeeding—at least enough for David to keep his attention off his phone.

Outside, I inched my car into a hidden corner of the loading dock, out of view from the upper windows. I killed the engine. The building seemed dauntingly silent. If David was tracking me through the phone's GPS, he'd see me close by but might assume I'd enter through the main lobby. I intended to do anything but that.

The stench of trash wafted on the faint wind as I opened my car door, bracing myself for what lay ahead. My eyes swept the perimeter for a service entrance. There a dented metal door marked "Authorized Personnel Only." Perfect. If I could reach it undetected, I might get the drop on David. But first, I took a second to gather my nerve. Laura and Adam were depending on me, and David's monstrous track record hinted he was beyond reason.

I turned my walkies' volume even lower. I couldn't afford Bruce's frantic yelling giving me away. The phones' GPS signals remained on, though. David's overconfidence could be the key to cornering him; he believed he had the entire city under his watch.

The next phase was about to begin. With any luck, Laura and Adam were finding a way to keep David distracted, feeding him enough arrogance to blind him from my approach and I prayed that approach would be swift enough to spare their lives.

I could see rage igniting behind David's eyes, and he was barely holding it together. Laura must have seen it too she shot me a small, triumphant smile, a look that made David's anger escalate further. It was as though his entire body quivered, ready to explode from the force of his fury.

"How does it feel this time to be the one getting chased?" I asked, my voice dripping with the same scorn he'd shown us. "You've always hunted people down in secret, picking them off in cowardly ways never giving them a real fight, I bet."

David's teeth clenched. Laura seized on the opening; her gaze fixed on him. "You're not some unstoppable killer, David. You're just a man who was a terrible lover too. I was never satisfied nobody was. Maybe that's why you killed them… because they refused to see you the way you wanted."

Her words were ice-cold deliberately aimed below the belt. I almost had to stifle a laugh, because it was so brutal, so precisely calculated to wound him where it hurt most. But it worked. David's nostrils flared; he was trembling with rage, eyes darting between us instead of checking his phone for Peter's location. All I could do was hope Peter's plan was taking shape in the background, giving him time to make his move.

Suddenly, David snapped. "Enough!" he roared, slamming a fist against the table. "I'm going to gut both of you when this is over after I kill Peter in front of your eyes. Then you'll see who's better once and for all. Shit, what the…?"

His tirade broke off as he glanced at his phone screen. A flicker of confusion contorted his features, a mix of dread and anger draining the color from his face. He stalked around the room, muttering and cursing under his breath, clearly wrestling with his next step.

Without warning, he spun on his heels and bolted from the conference room, leaving us alone. A tense silence fell in his wake.

That bastard is in the building no doubt. But I'm reading three separate signals. Did he actually scatter those phones on different floors? Damn it, I lost my focus. These two idiots got under my skin, and now I have no idea which signal is the real one. Well played, Peter… well played. But I'm not done. I'll kill all of you, no matter where you hide.

Checking the phone again, David noted the exact floors where he was picking up signals: 42, 43, and 44 all below his current position on the 45th.

Fine. He wants to play hide-and-seek. I'll head to 42 first, then work my way up, taking out each phone and Peter if I run into him. After I finish, I'll come back for Laura and Adam. Nobody humiliates me and lives.

My lungs burned from sprinting up the stairwell, past the 45th floor. I wanted to be above David once he started descending, so I'd have the advantage. Planting the last phone and an extra walkie on the 44th floor was nerve-racking, but crucial. With each phone placed on a different floor, David would be forced to guess where I really was.

I slipped quietly up the steps leading to the roof access, heart pounding. I didn't actually plan to go onto the roof just needed to wait near the 45th-floor door in the stairwell. If David tried to chase my false signals, he'd head down first. By the time he realized the trap, I'd be coming from above with the literal high ground.

There he is. Through the narrow window in the stairwell door, I saw David burst out onto the landing and hurry down the steps, phone in hand, frustration etched on his face. He was going after one of the decoy signals. Perfect.

Now, I just had to move fast enough to reach Adam and Laura before David doubled back or discovered the ruse. Taking a steadying breath, I turned the knob and slipped onto the 45th floor, determined to end this nightmare and save my friends.

"Okay, let's see what you've planned for me, Peter…" I muttered under my breath, stepping onto the forty-second floor. According to the phone's GPS, the first signal was right here. The corridor was dim, dust motes drifting through the stale air. If the old Exxon Tower had once been pristine and bustling, it was now a concrete relic—long shadows and peeling paint hinting at years of abandonment.

Sure enough, the blue dot on my screen led me to a deserted bathroom. I pushed open the door and flicked on my flashlight. Tiles were cracked, and the mirrors streaked with grime. It reeked faintly of old mildew. There on the edge of a rust-stained sink—lay one of Peter's phones, screen face-down like a discarded toy. Nobody was hiding in the stalls, nobody ready to jump out. Just a lonely phone.

"Tricky bastard," I hissed, snatching it up. "Not here to greet me, huh? Fine. On to the next one."

I headed for the stairwell, jogging down a short flight of steps toward the forty-third floor. My mind flashed to a half-memory of an Instagram post I'd seen from that "Nighthawkhouston" guy pictures of the tower's abandoned offices and conference rooms. Now I was seeing them in real time: the same drab carpet, the same broken cubicles… each floor felt like walking through ghostly snapshots.

Sure enough, the second phone was waiting on an ancient, dusty desk in some nameless office. "Marco Polo," I thought, ironically. Peter was leading me on a wild chase, each phone luring me to an empty place. I clenched my jaw in frustration. "Very cunning, Peter," I growled to the silent room. "But I've got one more phone to find—and you."

Pocketing phone number two, I stomped back to the stairs, climbing with renewed determination to the forty-fourth floor. If this last device was also deserted, then I'd know Peter was waiting on the forty-fifth with Laura and Adam.

I moved quietly but quickly along the corridor of the forty-fifth floor, the musty air thick with disuse. My mind flashed to the images on "Nighthawkhouston"'s Instagram—photos of the very floors I'd just booby-trapped with phones. But all thoughts of abandoned offices fell away the moment I opened the conference room door and saw Laura and Adam—bound but alive.

Their smiles lit up the dim room, and my heart soared as though a massive weight had been lifted from my shoulders. Without thinking, I ran to Laura and pulled her into a fierce hug, pressing a relieved kiss to her lips. Then I turned to Adam, yanking him into a playful bear hug, rocking side to side in that affectionate, exaggerated way guys do.

"Okay, I see how it is," Adam teased, once I'd released him. "Laura gets the first kiss, and I'm just sloppy seconds?"

We all laughed, a sharp but welcome burst of joy. It felt surreal to be joking when David could burst in at any moment, but we needed that moment of relief—a tiny taste of hope after everything we'd endured.

Laura's eyes sparkled with gratitude. "If it's not too much trouble, could you untie us, honey?" she asked, a mischievous lilt in her voice.

I raised an eyebrow. "Honey, huh? Looks like I'm taking on a new role. And poor Adam's just the third wheel now," I said with mock pity, untying them as fast as I could.

"Okay, jokes aside," I said, face flushing with a mixture of relief and embarrassment, "here's what's going on. I planted three phones on floors 42, 43, and 44, each one broadcasting its location. David's been following those signals, so he'll check each floor, thinking I'm at one of them. While he's doing that, I slipped up here to free you."

"That matches what Adam and I suspected," Laura said, stretching her wrists now that the ropes were gone. "He was so enraged after we taunted him, he forgot to keep checking his phone for a while. We figured that was you pulling some sort of trick."

"You guys nailed it," Adam chimed in. "So, you bought enough time to scatter those phones. But what's next?"

"That is the next part of the plan," I explained. "I've got a walkie on me, and I left another walkie on the forty-fourth floor right by the last phone. I know David will find it and try to call me out assuming it's me. Meanwhile, my boss has a walkie as well, all set to channel four. When David picks up that walkie and tries to talk, he'll be talking to both me and my boss at the same time, whether he realizes it or not."

Adam's brows shot up. "So, Bruce will finally hear David's voice?"

I nodded. "And hopefully enough of his ranting to learn exactly who he is and what he's done. Bruce wanted to do this by the book, but we both know David would kill you two the second he sensed a SWAT team in the halls. This way, maybe we can corner him from multiple angles."

"Well," Laura said, massaging her stiff shoulders, "I hope your plan works. David's not exactly the calm, rational type."

"He's dangerous, but he's also proud," I said, crossing my arms. "If we rattle him enough, he'll want to talk he's obsessed with proving he's superior. That's where the walkie and his own ego come in. Once he's too busy monologuing, it'll be our chance to strike… or get out."

For a moment, we just looked at one another, the gravity of the situation pressing in. We were all breathing faster than normal, minds racing. David was somewhere below us—and he'd soon realize I wasn't on any of those lower floors.

"Okay," Laura said quietly. "Let's do this."

With a collective breath, we steeled ourselves. David would be arriving soon, phones in tow, fury no doubt boiling over. We just had to make sure we were ready for him—and that this final confrontation would end on our terms.

I'm not entirely sure why I'm agreeing to play this game under Peter's conditions. Back in Greece, during one of my travels, I had a victim who was just as much trouble, constantly running, hiding, thinking he might escape. He didn't. When I finally caught him, the satisfaction felt like a ravenous thirst being quenched—the sort of hunger that builds and builds until the moment of relief arrives, and everything tastes richer, more intense. Right now, my plan is to kill Peter, Laura, and Adam, and I can almost feel that buffet of delight waiting for me. Three strong-willed, elusive people, each a trophy for my ongoing hunt. Maybe the media's label of "Code-Blooded Killer" is appropriate, because I've cracked the code of what makes life truly exhilarating: to live is to kill, to take something sacred and end it like a god deciding fates. A final demonstration of absolute power.

I found the last phone the third one on the forty-fourth floor, just where the signal said it would be. Next to it lay a two-way radio. Perfect. Peter's next invitation. Clearly, he wants to talk.

Back in the Conference Room

A sudden burst of static shot through the walkie we held, and time froze. Laura, Adam, and I locked eyes, our hearts pounding in unison, braced for whatever David would say.

David (through the walkie): "Hey, Peter. Looks like you're the one controlling the board now, scattering all these game pieces. Let's talk like civilized men. No need for me to kill Laura and Adam provided we can come to an understanding. Where are you?"

Peter: "You're not going to kill Laura or Adam, David. I'm right here with them, and they're free now. You are in checkmate. Also, my boss is on this channel. Chief Bruce Scott knows you're the 'Code-Blooded Killer.'"

Bruce (from the precinct): "David, this is Chief Scott. We've got you. Turn yourself in make it easy on everyone."

David: "I just want to talk. Then I promise I'll surrender hand myself over to Peter, personally. You have my word."

Bruce: "Alright, but don't let him out of your sight, Peter. If he twitches, put him down."

Peter lowered the walkie's volume, shooting us a cryptic look. Laura and I exchanged a glance, too. It felt like there was another layer to this plan—one we weren't fully privy to. The tension in the room was overwhelming, like we were reading the final lines of a story that could twist in any direction.

"Don't worry," Peter said quietly, noticing our concern. "We've got him. I want to end this once and for all."

Almost on cue, a knock echoed from the conference room door. Laura's spine stiffened; Adam's breath caught. Was David actually being courteous? Polite? Or was this some twisted mind game?

David (on the other side of the door): "I come in peace," he joked. "But, well, yes I'm holding a gun, because you have a gun too, Peter."

Peter: "Drop your weapon, David. You said you wanted to talk, and holding a gun isn't exactly friendly."

David: "Fine, I'm a man of my word. I'll put mine on the table. But why don't you put yours on the table, too? No guns in hand just a civil meeting. This used to be a prestigious corporate boardroom, making big decisions that affected the world. Now it's a place to decide all our lives. I'd say that's even more important."

With our hearts thundering, we watched as David nudged the door open. He stepped in cautiously, gun raised but not aimed, then placed it on the table with deliberate slowness. Peter looked back at us Laura and Adam and we sensed the same question in his stare: Can we trust him not to shoot the second we drop our guard?

Still, Peter exhaled and set his own handgun on the polished, dust-coated surface, sliding it just out of his immediate reach. The old corporate conference room had once hosted high-stakes deals, but nothing like this. The overhead lights flickered, casting shadows across the scattered chairs and the tense faces confronting one another.

David walked calmly to the conference table and, with deliberate showmanship, slid his gun across its surface. It scraped to a stop at least an arm's length away—making a point that he didn't plan to grab for it anytime soon. Still, his smile suggested he was very much in control. Peter stepped over, placed his gun down beside David's, then took a seat to David's left. Laura followed, settling in next to Peter. I ended up on David's right, so the four of us formed a semicircle around the end of the table, as though we were kicking off a routine board meeting.

"Anyone mind if I smoke?" David asked, already reaching into his coat pocket.

"Go ahead," Peter responded warily. "No one's stopping you.

A soft chuckle escaped David's lips as he retrieved a cigarette. "Too bad this isn't the sixties. If we were in some 'Mad Men' scenario, I'd have a tumbler of bourbon to go with my smoke. Corporations and agencies used to do that, I hear—booze in the office, chain-smoking during meetings. Hard to picture it nowadays, but back then, I guess they made world-changing decisions while half buzzed."

He flicked a lighter, the brief flare casting shifting shadows across his features. For a moment, the only sound was the sizzle of tobacco as he inhaled. The incongruity of it a man who'd killed countless people chatting about old-time corporate culture made my stomach tighten.

"Is this really what you want to talk about, David?" Laura asked bluntly, breaking the tension. "Just… idle bullshit?"

David exhaled smoke, tilting his head. "Alright, fair enough. You want to skip the small talk. I was just warming up, but if you'd rather jump straight to the serious stuff…" His eyes flicked from Laura to Peter, and finally landed on me.

I swallowed hard, then ventured a question. "Why all of this?" I asked, keeping my gaze on him. "You killed so many people before you even met Laura. Then after she left you, you went back to killing again. Why?"

Adam's Reflection

I'd heard pieces of David's story, having spent the last few days tied up in this very room, forced to listen to his convoluted justifications. Yet everything still felt blurred by moral grayness and twisted logic. David had described his travels, how he'd slaughtered men across the globe, and the "why" always boiled down to a strange hunger for control or purpose. But what did that even mean? So many innocent lives taken—for what? A man's ego? Some misguided search for meaning?

Whenever someone kills, we instinctively want the act to have some reason, as if murder must be tied to some deeper logic. But maybe, for David, it was just a matter of impulse—a reflex. We're surrounded by billions of people we'll never meet or care about. If you don't value human life, maybe you just… destroy it.

David flicked a bit of ash from his cigarette onto the table, seeming almost thoughtful. His casual posture made it all the more unsettling—like he was mulling over what to say, how much to admit, or whether to spin some grand philosophy we'd find horrifying.

He let out a slow breath of smoke, tapping the ash onto an old coffee-stained coaster abandoned on the table. "Innocent or not," he began, "that's a label you're slapping on them. I never saw it that way. You want to hear me say it's because I'm crazy, or I had some traumatic childhood, or that I found a twisted calling? Maybe. I've done a lot of thinking, ironically enough. And I keep circling back to the same truth: I like to kill."

He paused, eyes scanning our reactions—Laura clenching her fists, Peter tense and ready to lunge, me just sitting there, heart pounding in my chest.

"Don't get me wrong," David continued, "I'm not discounting the thrill of it. There's a power in deciding who lives and who dies. And once you realize you can do it—and get away with it why stop? This world is so large, and no one truly cares about a few random strangers dying, not until the body count hits the headlines. And for me…" He shrugged. "Traveling, seeing the variety of life, made it easy to find new targets. People want to blame my so-called addiction on trauma, or call me a psycho. Fine. But for me, it's about freedom. To do what I want. To live as I see fit."

He cracked a mirthless grin, looking toward Laura. "Then I met you, and I paused. For a moment, I thought maybe there's something else—another high. You were different, but eventually, you left, and that… that was a step back to what I do best."

Laura's face hardened; she leaned forward. "You left me no choice," she hissed, voice trembling. "It was like seeing a monster's mask slip knowing what you were capable of, even if I didn't know all the details. I couldn't stay."

David lifted his cigarette to his lips again, letting the smoke curl around him. "I respect that," he said softly. "You recognized what I am. But I'm not going to apologize. I am this. And I'll keep being this until something someone stops me. Is that you, Peter?"

Confrontation at the Table

Peter planted his elbows on the table, hands clasped. "Yeah," he said quietly, "I'm here to stop you, David. And I'm not alone. My boss, Chief Scott—he's hearing everything. We have walkies, we have plans… you're cornered. This ends tonight."

David's gaze flickered to the guns on the table—his and Peter's. For a moment, he looked like he might grab one, but then he casually nudged them both further away with the side of his forearm.

"If it ends tonight," he said, flicking his cigarette ash onto the coaster again, "then at least I made a good run of it. But you see, Peter… I still don't think you have what it takes to kill me. Your hesitation will be your downfall."

Peter straightened, a muscle ticking in his jaw. "I have no problem doing what I must," he said. "You've killed my friends, threatened my life, tortured Adam, and kidnapped Laura someone I…" His voice caught for a second, then he forced it steady. "Someone I love. If you think I'll hesitate, you're wrong."

A tense silence followed, the air thick with the scent of smoke and the tang of raw adrenaline. Outside, the hum of the city's nighttime traffic reached us faintly through the building's old windows. If the old Exxon Tower's walls could talk, they'd bear witness to a twisted story far more surreal than any corporate meeting it once hosted.

Finally, David stubbed his cigarette out on the coaster, letting out a final puff of smoke. "Then I guess we see who blinks first," he said, leaning back in his seat, arms splayed as though he owned the place.

Laura and I exchanged uneasy glances. The tension in the room felt like a coiled spring, each of us aware that the slightest flicker of movement, the slightest shift in tone, could spark an eruption of violence. David's truths were out in the open he enjoyed killing, he'd do it again if not stopped. And now it all hinged on Peter's plan… or a single moment of action.

David leaned forward, resting his elbows on the conference table and glancing around at the three of us Laura, Peter, and me like a manager about to deliver an all-hands speech. He exhaled softly, almost as if calming himself, then turned to me with a thin smile.

"I told you some of this before, Adam," he said. "But I haven't shared it with your dear friends yet. Maybe you never fully understood, or I rambled too much to make it relatable."

Laura's patience was wearing thin. "Keep it short and to the point."

David let out a short laugh, tapping his fingertips on the table's dusty surface. "Yes, yes. To the point."

The way David spoke reminded me of a grandstanding manager who thinks his every word is revelatory, like some street-corner preacher drawing a crowd. Except in this scenario, we were his captive audience three blind mice, as he liked to call us—and he was the self-appointed prophet of his own serial-killer doctrine.

"Alright," he began, letting his voice drop slightly. "Here's the core truth of who I am. A single moment shaped me—like a seed planted deep in my mind that grew into the… person you see now. I suppose everyone has a memory or event so powerful; it cements itself in your consciousness forever. It becomes the turning point. For me, it happened when I was a teenager, riding in a car with my dad."

He paused for a breath, glancing around the former corporate boardroom as if he were gauging its ambiance. The overhead lights hummed faintly, casting stale light over the scattered chairs and dusty table.

"I remember all those drives," David continued. "Car rides. School bus rides. Back and forth across town. Different roads, different routes… but none of them seemed to matter. They were just…" He shrugged. "Dim experiences. Faded visuals. A routine I barely acknowledged."

Laura folded her arms, her posture rigid, but David didn't seem to mind her obvious discomfort.

"Then one day," he said, "I had this… epiphany. I realized I needed to feel everything—physically, mentally, emotionally. Call me a 'texture eater,' if you will. I like to experience the difference between mashed potatoes and French fries… the same basic food, but totally different sensations. That epiphany drove me to want more of life's textures—the kind you only really notice when your body is in motion, doing something. So, I started running every route I'd taken by car or bus, re-claiming them with my own feet. It wasn't a sad 'Forrest Gump' run. It was about reclaiming lost moments, about not letting machines do all my living for me."

He paused for effect, letting his gaze wander between each of us. A faint smoke residue still lingered in the air from his earlier cigarette, giving the room an even more claustrophobic feel.

"That car-ride epiphany," David went on, "led me to… well, eventually everything else I've done. I traveled the world, seeking intense experiences. Yes, I got distracted, numbing myself on cheap thrills. But then came my first kill in Cambodia."

A hush fell over us. We all knew he'd bragged about Cambodia before, about the moment it clicked for him.

"Getting held up by a mugger, ironically," David said, "in a dark alley. I had a choice: give in or fight back. That's when my mind kicked into overdrive—time slowed down, and I felt this… awakening. That's what I'd been missing. That primal sense of control, the adrenaline, the living in the moment. My epiphany from that day of running suddenly fused with my instincts: if I could take a life, I'd truly be in command of my own."

He exhaled, a faint smirk twisting his lips, as though the memory stirred a faint pleasure in him. "Maybe it's a survival mechanism humans have—time warps, your brain yanks forward every past experience to help you deal with a threat. But for me, it became a lust. I had found my purpose. This is who I am."

Laura's jaw tightened, her eyes bright with anger—and perhaps a twinge of sorrow that she'd once let this man into her life. Adam—the "me" in this scenario—could sense the tension in every muscle, the confusion raging between disbelief and horror. Peter had both hands braced on the tabletop, knuckles white, glancing toward the guns we'd set aside but never truly forgotten.

"So that's it," I managed to say. "You realized you liked killing people—felt it in your bones and made it your calling?"

David spread his palms in a what-can-you-do gesture. "Life is short," he replied. "Some climb mountains for the rush, some chase fame. I chase the ultimate thrill: deciding life or death. Don't look so shocked. Humans do it every day just more… systematically."

He leaned back in his chair, eyes gleaming with a cold, calm rationality at odds with the monstrous acts he'd confessed to. "Sure, you can argue I'm insane," he said. "But I see it differently. I embrace experience, from a small jolt of flavor in my mouth to the rush of taking a life. It's raw. It's real. More honest than any polite, corporate façade."

Peter sucked in a breath, fighting to keep his composure. "And that's why you targeted Laura, and Adam, and me… because you wanted a bigger challenge, right? Another intense experience?"

David tilted his head, considering. "You might say so. Once Laura walked away, I realized I wasn't done. You three, you're… interesting. You fight back. That makes it more potent. A little cat-and-mouse with high stakes."

He flashed a smile that didn't reach his eyes, then turned slightly, addressing Laura directly. "So, my dear Laura, does that 'answer' your question? Are you satisfied hearing the short version? Or do you want me to tie it up with a moral at the end?"

The question hung as thick as the smoky haze. Laura's lips parted, but no words came out. The lines of her face said enough: she was revolted, furious, and maybe just a little heartbroken that she'd ever cared about someone so fundamentally broken. I caught Peter's eye. A single nod passed between us, an unspoken agreement that the time for talk was nearly done.

David saw that, too. His grin broadened, though his fingers tapped restlessly on the table. We were all waiting for the next move his or ours. He'd had his say, laid out his twisted logic. Now it was up to us to dismantle it… or him.

Outside the conference room windows, the city lights glowed in the evening sky. Once, executives had gathered here to shape business deals and corporate expansions. Now, we were shaping something far more final a showdown that would end one life or change many. And by the look in David's eyes, he was betting it would be ours.

I pictured myself grabbing his knife and killing him—plain and simple. That image flashed through my mind, spurred by an electric jolt of physical, mental, and emotional energy. In a single heartbeat, I felt ready to act, certain with every cell in my body that this was what it meant to be fully alive again—more so even than when I used to run those routes, testing my limits in both mind and muscle. I felt how my life was taking another life, how it meant power and control, how it laid bare the human capacity to contemplate existence and then extinguish it. Billions of years in the universe, and these few seconds were a mere nano-speck slipping away. **Life was meaningful and meaningless all at once—**we came from nothing, and we left in the same emptiness.

"Okay," Peter said, tone dry, "that definitely wasn't short or to the point. You killed because you wanted to feel something, with no consequences, no morals. I'm not sure which country wants first crack at frying your ass, but I'm sure they'll all want a piece."

Some people just aren't meant to live in this world. It comes down to doing your best not to ruin yourself or others along the way, and David grinning at his own story made it clear he didn't fit with the rest of us.

"Mind if I grab another smoke?" he asked, hand already sliding into his jacket.

As he pulled out a cigarette, we saw the switchblade glint under the lights. All at once, we froze again our guns too far away on the table to be any help. David must have relished that moment of shock.

"Yeah, those guns won't save you," he said, almost amused. "Relax. I'm not talented enough to kill all three of you with this little knife. But this—" he turned the blade so we caught the polished glare "is the one I got off that guy in Cambodia. I can still feel what it was like to shove it into his brain. Now, I'll feel that same rush ending my own life. Living and deciding my own exit that's real control."

We watched, speechless, as David took one final drag, blowing the smoke from deep in his lungs. Then he raised the knife the same knife he'd killed so many with and pressed it to his right temple. Slowly, deliberately, he slid the blade deep into his head. He slumped forward onto the old corporate desk, his body collapsing as if someone had flicked a switch. The desk, like everything else in this deserted conference room, suddenly felt haunted by his final act.

For a while, Peter, Laura, and I said nothing, staring with a numb sense of disbelief at David's lifeless form. None of us dared move; we each kept to our own space as though we'd set invisible boundaries we couldn't cross. The silence ended only when Peter turned on his walkie, letting the static and chaotic buzz fill the stale air, which still carried the tang of David's cigarette smoke.

"Bruce," Peter said, his voice oddly hollow, "the killer's dead. He… killed himself. Bring a team up here and take the body."

Later days

A strange undercurrent in life hides beneath the surface, always waiting for the moment when you think you're on solid ground then it drags you into a swirl of doubt and confusion. Saying we were disoriented after everything that happened with David is an understatement. Even after all this time, his words still echo in my mind, as though they've fused with my subconscious. I find myself circling those memories whenever I drift off to sleep, replaying every conversation like a worn-out tape caught in a loop.

Laura and Peter, on the other hand, seem to have found a stronger connection. Everything they went through somehow made them more resilient and more in love. In my case, I feel drained, like I've turned into an old battery that can't quite charge back to a full hundred percent. When you're scarred, it's as if a piece of you is replaced by something that never feels quite the same.

Sometimes, we get stuck in our own heads, second-guessing ourselves and doubting we can connect with anyone else. That was me for a long while after we walked out of the Exxon Tower. Modern psychologists would probably stamp it with a label like PTSD. But to me, it was just the same old emotional weight, the same churn of thoughts under a different name.

And it doesn't help that living in a new city can make you feel like a foreigner in your own country. Every city has its own personality some wild, some tame. Houston felt more like a restless beast, all concrete and glass, barely giving you room to breathe. It gave me a kind of cabin fever, urging me to keep moving. I never felt like it was my final stop, just a way station before heading somewhere else.

Yet somehow, eight months slipped by. I'd wake up on Saturdays, my head buzzing with questions I might never answer, only to realize how much time had passed since David disappeared from our lives. Laura, Peter, and I hardly talked about it, but we all had our own paths we were walking quietly, without fanfare, waiting to see where they led.

Eventually, the three of us agreed to meet up at our favorite coffee place, a space that felt comfortably routine. Even if we hadn't said it out loud, I was sure the conversation would turn to everything we'd been holding back. Maybe that was the point sometimes you keep silent until you're ready to face the truth. With coffee and familiarity as a backdrop, it felt like the right time to acknowledge the past and figure out where we were headed next.

"Howdy!" I said, arriving late. Peter and Laura were already seated, sipping their coffees as if they had all the time in the world.

"Don't worry about your coffee, pal," Peter said, smiling. "I got your large black one here exactly how you like it."

"Oh, you shouldn't have, honey," I joked, matching his playful tone.

Laura joined in. "Alright, you two can get a room if you want, but I'm staying put."

It felt good to be around them no matter how long we'd been apart, that natural ease in our friendship was still there, never forced.

"So," I teased, "Laura, would you mind if I borrow Peter for a while? We're talking free love here, right?"

She winked at me. "He's all yours. I need a break."

I laughed, then decided to change the subject. "Anyway, I actually have some news for you guys."

"Well, we've got news too," Peter and Laura chimed in at the same time.

I glanced between them. "We? Did you rehearse that? But go ahead—two people with a shared announcement outranks one guy's lonely story."

Laura grinned, nudging Peter's arm. "Peter got a job in Bishop—he's going to be their new sheriff!"

Peter nodded. "With all the press surrounding the 'Code-Blooded Killer,' plus my family's history in Bishop law enforcement… they've been asking me to come back for a while. It felt like the right time to say yes."

"That's amazing!" I told them both. "I'm really happy for you—so, wedding bells next, huh?"

Peter raised a hand, mock-serious. "Whoa, slow down there, partner. We're not splitting up, but we are taking it one step at a time—figuring out how Bishop and California feel as our new home."

I glanced at Laura, checking if she was cool with Peter's joke. She just smiled, no hint of offense. It was clear they were on the same page.

"Alright, your turn," she prompted me.

I took a breath. "I'm not sure how to say this…"

Peter cut in, grinning. "Let me guess—show you how good a sheriff I'll be: You're going to the CIA."

My jaw dropped. "What? How'd you know that?"

He shrugged, clearly pleased with himself. "I got a call a while back—part of their reference checks. They asked all kinds of questions about your character, so I told them the worst dirt I could think of. But apparently, you still passed."

"You jerk!" Laura laughed, tossing a napkin at him.

Peter raised his hands, still grinning. "I'm kidding, pal. You deserve it. I knew for a while but waited for you to share. I think you'll be a great CIA agent."

"Thank you," I said, exhaling the relief that came with saying it out loud. "It feels good to go home, back East. It's not North Carolina, but Williamsburg, Virginia will still feel like home."

"We leave next week," Laura said, leaning into Peter. "How about you?"

"Same," I replied. "Next week, it's off to a new life. I guess I won't be a geologist anymore."

For a moment, the three of us paused, letting the significance sink in. We were all on the edge of something different new towns, new roles, new possibilities. And somehow, it felt right that we were sharing the news over coffee, just like we always had.